SWALLOWBROOK'S WEDDING OF THE YEAR

BY
ABIGAIL GORDON

MILLS &
BOON

First published in Great Britain 2013
by Mills & Boon, an imprint of Harlequin (UK) Limited.
Harlequin (UK) Limited, Eton House,
18-24 Paradise Road, Richmond, Surrey TW9 1SR

© Abigail Gordon 2013

ISBN: 978 0 263 89879 8

Abigail Gordon loves to write about the fascinating combination of medicine and romance from her home in a Cheshire village. She is active in local affairs, and is even called upon to write the script for the annual village pantomime! Her eldest son is a hospital manager, and helps with all her medical research. As part of a close-knit family, she treasures having two of her sons living close by, and the third one not too far away. This also gives her the added pleasure of being able to watch her delightful grandchildren growing up.

Recent titles by the same author:

MARRIAGE MIRACLE IN SWALLOWBROOK**
SPRING PROPOSAL IN SWALLOWBROOK**
SWALLOWBROOK'S WINTER BRIDE**
SUMMER SEASIDE WEDDING†
THE VILLAGE NURSE'S HAPPY-EVER-AFTER†
WEDDING BELLS FOR THE VILLAGE NURSE†
CHRISTMAS IN BLUEBELL COVE†
COUNTRY MIDWIFE, CHRISTMAS BRIDE*

**The Doctors of Swallowbrook Farm
*The Willowmere Village Stories
†Bluebell Cove

**These books are also available in eBook format
from www.millsandboon.co.uk**

FOR GILL AND PHILIP AND CREATIVE WRITING

CHAPTER ONE

A TAXI had pulled up on the forecourt of the medical practice in the Lakeland village of Swallowbrook and as its driver unloaded baggage out of the boot, his passenger, a tall guy with russet hair bleached by a foreign sun and with a tan that spoke of long days beneath it, eased himself out of the vehicle and looked around him.

He could see a lake not far away with a backdrop of the rugged fells that were so much a part of the area where he had grown up and then five years ago had left in turmoil, vowing that he never wanted to see or hear of the place ever again.

That was how it had been until he'd phoned to have a chat with a colleague, Nathan Gallagher, who had worked at the same African hospital as himself and was now back in the UK.

When Nathan had arrived on a three-year contract at the hospital where *he himself* had already been established, they'd discovered that they had been born in the same English county and had grown up only a few miles from each other.

It had created a bond between them that hadn't been

broken when the other man, having completed his contract, had returned home, leaving himself with still a year to do. Now that year was up and, like his friend before him, he'd returned to the UK.

'Aaron!' a voice cried from somewhere behind him. 'You're here at last!' As Aaron Somerton swung round to greet Nathan he saw that he had emerged as one of a group of people leaving a new building on the same plot of land as the Swallowbrook medical practice.

As they shook hands Nathan turned to a couple standing nearby and said, 'Allow me to introduce Laura Armitage, our practice manager, and her husband, Gabriel, who is an oncologist and about to take over the running of the new building that you see beside you, which has only today been opened as an extension for cancer care in the area.'

'So are you the lady who has found me that delightful cottage to live in?' Aaron asked with a smile for Laura.

'Yes,' she replied, 'and if you would like to come to my office in the basement beneath the surgery I'll give you the keys to The Falls Cottage, which, as the title suggests, is near a waterfall.'

Leaving Nathan and Gabriel chatting, Laura took him through the practice building to the office where she worked amongst the computers, and on observing that there were no staff to be seen on the premises he commented on the fact.

'The surgery is closed this afternoon,' she told him, 'so that our staff could attend the opening of the clinic.

Most of them are over there now, enjoying the refreshments that have been provided.'

When they rejoined her husband and Nathan, who was head of the practice, Aaron asked, 'How soon do you want me on the job, Nathan?'

'As soon as possible,' he was told, 'but take a couple of days to settle in first. Swallowbrook will no doubt seem strange to you after such a long absence from these parts, even though it is changeless in many ways.'

The taxi had gone and he said, 'I'll take you to the cottage as I'm sure you must be keen to see it, and by the way, Aaron, my wife, Libby, says if you would like to dine with us tonight, you are very welcome.'

Seated at a table by a window in the restaurant of the new clinic with the other two nurses from the surgery, Julianne Marshall had seen the taxi arrive outside the practice building and was watching its occupant emerge.

Why had he come back? she wondered with a sick feeling in the pit of her stomach. The last words she'd heard Aaron Somerton speak before he'd disappeared five years ago had been to declare that he never wanted to set eyes on the Lakeland valley where he'd lived, or the people in it, ever again, and he'd meant it. No doubt about that!

When Laura Armitage's husband, the dishy Gabriel, had appeared on the scene she'd thought that he was going to fill the vacancy at the practice that had arisen when Nathan's wife, Libby, also a doctor, had left to become a full-time mother.

Keen to know if she was right in her surmise, she'd questioned Nathan and been told that a guy called Aaron Somerton, who had been working in Africa for the last five years, was coming to fill the gap, and Julianne had thought she was going to collapse.

Now he was here, only yards away, and she was hoping desperately that he wouldn't recognise her. She'd watched Laura take him into the practice building and thought if it hadn't been for the opening of the clinic today she would have been a sitting duck, unable to avoid meeting him on his unexpected return to the area where it had all happened in what seemed like a lifetime ago. A lifetime that had been like serving a sentence for something she hadn't done.

Yet if she didn't meet him today, it was going to happen tomorrow. There was no way she could escape it, unless she rang in sick or disappeared off the face of the earth, like Aaron had done.

She watched Nathan drive off with him in his car and assumed that the head of the practice would be taking the new arrival to the cottage that had been rented for him by the side of the waterfall that, fed by streams and rainwater from the fells, surged endlessly downwards into the lake.

It would be a far more atmospheric residence than her apartment above the village bakery on the main street, but did that really matter? If Aaron Somerton recognised her, he wasn't likely to be coming round for tea.

* * *

The cottage was exactly how Aaron had expected it to be.

Like almost every property in the area, it was built from Lakeland stone, which was charming in itself, but added to that was the fact that it was actually at the lake edge, only feet away from where the waterfall came dancing down from the fells.

It was described as a cottage, which brought to mind something small and cosy, but was far from that. The rooms were spacious and attractive, with huge windows looking out onto impressive views of the area, and thankfully the church didn't appear in any of them. He would have had to draw the curtains if it had.

When he'd rung Nathan that night for a chat and his friend had suggested that he fill the vacancy at the Swallowbrook practice if he was intending to come back to the UK, nothing had been further from his mind, yet recklessly he'd taken him up on the offer, and ever since had been looking forward to returning to his roots, with all the bad memories firmly buttoned down at the back of his mind.

Both of his parents had died while he'd been at medical college so there had been no one close to him to share the most humiliating moment of his life, and the job in Africa had been heaven-sent as a means of escaping the notoriety that had been the result of him being jilted at the altar.

When sugar-sweet golden-haired Nadine Marshall had wanted to marry him, he had seen a future of heavenly bliss beckoning with the woman he loved and their children in time to come, and had had no idea that she'd been seeing someone else while the wedding preparations had been in progress.

On meeting up with Nathan in Africa there had been no mention about what had happened on his wedding day, so either the other man knew nothing about it or didn't connect his caring, clever colleague with the time when Aaron had been hurt beyond belief by Nadine and had gone to work at the other side of the world to try to forget.

Now he was back in the land of his birth, amongst the lakes and fells that were as familiar to him as his own face, hoping that his rash decision to come back to Swallowbrook and the surrounding areas wasn't going to turn out to be a step too far.

He needed food, he decided when he'd finished unpacking—bread, milk, cereals, butter, bacon and anything else that caught his attention in the village shops, which were near enough for him to reach on foot.

The bakery was his last stopping place and as he opened the door and stepped inside he saw a neat pair of ankles and legs that were long and shapely in sheer tights disappearing fast up a flight of stairs at the back of the shop. Someone was in a hurry and he wondered if the flash of a dark blue hemline belonged to a nurse.

As she hovered on an upstairs landing after her quick departure from the shop down below on seeing Aaron about to enter, Julianne was thinking dismally that it would have to come sooner or later, meeting him face-to-face.

If he didn't recognise the woman she had become, Aaron would certainly remember her second name, if not the first, as she'd been a background figure during the time he had courted her elder sister, Nadine, with eyes only for her beauty.

But *she* was the one who was going to have to face him day after day, week after week from now on. Not the despicable Nadine, who had broken his heart and his pride, but the bridesmaid who since then hadn't wanted to be anyone's bride.

Because if her sister hadn't loved Aaron Somerton, she had adored him from afar and had ended up as the whipping girl for his betrayal because he had decided that she'd been in cahoots with the woman who had left him standing before a church full of people, and his anger and disgust had remained like a festering sore on her life ever since.

Yet her dismay at Aaron's return was not absolute. In a small corner of her heart there was warmth because whatever the cost in days to come, Aaron was where she could see him, observe him from a distance, and maybe in time he might come to feel that she wasn't as bad as she'd been made to look.

She heard the shop door close down below and when she looked out of the window from the landing where she had taken refuge he was striding along the pavement below with his provisions, and as people passing observed him with interest she thought he was still an eye-turner like he had been in the past, but did he notice, did he care?

At that moment a horrible thought struck her. Supposing he had recovered from being jilted at the altar by a greedy and uncaring bride and had found himself a replacement while out in Africa? Supposing he had a family waiting for him at the cottage by the waterfall while he went to buy food for them?

Yet the memory of his arrival offered solace regarding that. He had been alone. The only baggage he'd brought with him had been of the suitcase kind.

Having made sure that he'd gone, Julianne went back downstairs to the bakery and middle-aged George, the baker, who kept a fatherly eye on his attractive tenant, enquired, 'What sent you up the stairs so fast? I thought the guy buying the bread must be a vampire with a preference for young nurses or something.'

'He's the new doctor at the practice,' she told him. 'It will be soon enough to meet him when I have to, and you, George, wouldn't know a vampire if one jumped up and bit you.'

'Cheeky wench,' he said affectionately, passing her the bread and cakes that she'd been on the point of buying when Aaron had appeared. 'Don't forget these. I don't want you ringing my bell when you come home in the early hours because you've got nothing to eat.'

Julianne was smiling until she entered her apartment and then gloom descended. It was Tuesday, music night at The Mallard, the pub at the opposite end of the village, and there was always a band performing. She and her friends were regulars, wouldn't miss it for anything, but today her anticipation was dwindling because of the day's events.

Yet she thought it was ridiculous to let a brief sighting of someone she'd known in the past make her want to run away and hide. She was going to stick to the arrangements she'd made with her friend Kathy and really dress up for the occasion to give her morale a boost.

'Wow! Who are you out to impress?' Kathy asked when Julianne took off her coat on entering The Mallard and the dress beneath it was revealed.

It was bright scarlet, low cut, with an uneven hemline of long and short tails, and it fitted as if she'd been poured into it. Black patent-leather shoes with incredible heels and a matching bag made up the rest of her outfit.

From the moment of arriving at the noisy gathering Julianne had put Aaron Somerton's presence in the village out of her mind for a few hours and was back to her usual self of the attractive party animal concentrating on enjoying herself with tomorrow hidden in mist.

Aaron had accepted Nathan and Libby's invitation to dine with them that evening and as he'd walked the short distance to where they'd had two cottages made into one across the way from the surgery, he'd heard loud music coming from the pub that was a favourite haunt for the young and trendy amongst the locals and the many visitors who came to Swallowbrook.

He smiled a grim smile. The last time he'd been to anywhere like that had been with the woman he'd been going to marry and they'd danced non-stop.

A couple of weeks later Nadine had changed her mind and left him standing dumbstruck at the altar as she'd run down the aisle with the flowers of her bouquet scattering behind her, broken like the promises she'd decided she didn't want to make.

He'd gone after her and had been just in time to see her clutching the folds of her dress and with her veil streaming out behind her, jump into a red sports car that was parked at the church gates with engine running.

The rest of it had been a blur—wedding guests commiserating awkwardly and then drifting off, the vicar offering gentle condolences and assuring him that he would be available for support at any time that he might need him. And he'd seen the young bridesmaid with eyes large in her face though not exactly dismayed, and wondered if she'd known anything about the sports-car guy and had been expecting his own public humiliation.

He'd never seen the sly young minx from that day to this after he'd taken her on one side and waltzed her into the church vestry, where he'd discovered on questioning that she'd tried to persuade her sister endlessly not to marry him; and must have eventually succeeded.

He hadn't waited to hear any more. It had been clear that she was just as devious as Nadine. Whatever he'd done to either of them to deserve that treatment he didn't know, and had declared that he never wanted to set eyes on the pair of them again as long as he lived.

But now, out of choice, he was back in Lakeland and ready to put his self-imposed absence behind him like a bad dream. He imagined that the bridesmaid would have found a husband of her own by now and moved on somewhere else, like Nadine had done, and if she had he hoped that she would treat him better than his treacherous bride had treated him.

With the position in Africa coming up, he'd packed his bags and gone, and had never laid his hands on another woman since, neither was likely to do so in the future. Money and glamour had been a better choice than love, he'd discovered where Nadine had been concerned, and he was never likely to tread *that* path again.

Nathan had offered to drive him back to The Falls Cottage after a very pleasant evening, but Aaron had assured him that he would enjoy the walk in the mellow darkness of a late autumn evening.

As he strolled back the way he had come he had to pass The Mallard again and this time it didn't bring back memories of times when he hadn't known his happiness was in the balance. It was just a rather noisy place where people were enjoying themselves, and why not?

It was late and he had to sidestep to avoid a group that had just left the place and were chatting on the pavement. His glance rested for a second on a girl in a red dress, slim, dark haired, dark eyed, who had turned away as he'd approached, and he wondered why.

He didn't sleep well that first night. The noise of the waterfall was something he was going to have to get used to, he thought as he went to stand beside it as it hurtled down in the moonlight.

The memory of the folks coming out of the pub happy and carefree was still there. He had almost forgotten how to enjoy himself since the body blow he'd received from his faithless fiancée had destroyed any inclination he might have had towards that sort of thing, and the work he had gone to do amongst the heat and endless health problems of a far country, though rewarding and challenging, had not helped to make him feel any less joyless.

Yet as he turned to go back inside he found he was smiling, his spirits lifting. He had done the right thing in coming back to this beautiful Lakeland, he told himself. The past was done with. He was not going to allow it to intrude into the future. He had survived what Nadine had done to him and from now on intended to be happy and carefree in his new surroundings.

He could see the shops on the main street in the distance and saw that late as it was there was a light on in the rooms above the bakery, so he wasn't the only one still up.

Back in her flat, Julianne was staring into space. The last thing she'd wanted had been to come face-to-face with Aaron outside The Mallard amongst the noise and laughter of its patrons at the end of an evening of dancing and drinking, and after the first moment of unexpected recognition she'd turned away, wishing that she was dressed in a colour less memorable than red.

If he had recognised her he would no doubt have seen scarlet as the right colour for any woman associated with Nadine. But he hadn't, and if she could escape any scrutiny that brought recognition when they came face-to-face at the surgery, she would be relieved beyond telling. If she didn't, then what? Leave and look for a position somewhere else?

Yet she would hate to have to do that as the only people in her life were the few casual friends she'd made since joining the practice. Her parents were divorced—her mother married for a second time and living in Australia, and her father spent his days as steward and general factotum on a luxury yacht that its owners spent their time sailing around the world in, so he only appeared rarely in her life.

As for her Nadine, she hadn't seen her since the day she'd left Aaron devastated at the altar and she had no wish to do so in the future. If he'd given her the chance during those moments when they'd been alone in the vestry she would have explained that her only reason for not being horrified at what her sister had done to him had been because she'd had a youthful crush on him and wished she could have been his bride instead.

She would have squirmed in the telling of it because compared to Nadine she'd been like an ugly duckling next to a beautiful swan in her teenage years and gauche with it.

But Aaron hadn't given her the chance and in a sick sort of way she'd been relieved to be saved the embarrassment of admitting such a thing to a man who barely knew she existed.

The only time they'd had any conversation before that had been once when he'd been waiting for Nadine to get ready to go partying. It had been at the flat that she and her sister had shared in the town centre as Nadine was no lover of the countryside, and she'd been forced to listen to how fortunate he felt he was to have someone so beautiful wanting to marry him.

At the time she'd been reminded of men who had tried to chat *her* up as a means of getting to know her golden-haired sister and how she'd sent them packing, but tongue-tied in his presence she'd refrained from offering a word of warning because she'd known that the envy of other men would only make Nadine more desirable in his eyes.

It had been a rich man who had used his wealth to tempt Nadine away from the altar that day. The thought of him waiting out there with all that he could give her had made her choose possessions before love.

Julianne had known that she was seeing someone else, and had begged her not to marry Aaron if she didn't love him, but Nadine's reply to that had been that she *did* love him, but Howie *was* very rich *and* he adored her.

With the selfishness that was so much a part of her, she had waited until Aaron had actually been at the altar before making her decision, and the hurt she'd caused had been indescribable.

With that bleak thought to end the day Julianne undressed and once beneath the covers tried not to think about what the future held. She was used to laughing a lot, playing a lot, should have been on the stage as most of it was acting a part. What sort of a performance was she going to have to put on working alongside Aaron Somerton?

When he'd disappeared into the unknown she'd never expected to see him again and part of her had been relieved, but for the rest there had been a yearning that had never gone away and now, unbelievably, he was back in her life, here in Swallowbrook!

Nathan had told him to take a couple of days to settle in before taking his place in the practice but Aaron felt the urge to be back practising medicine on his home soil, and when the staff began to arrive at the surgery he was amongst them, tall, tanned and white shirted, ready for the fray.

'You didn't have to come in today,' Nathan told him, pleasantly surprised. 'I did say take a couple of days to get settled in.'

'Yes, I know,' Aaron replied. 'But I was settled as soon as I saw the lake and the rest of the village. I had no intention of ever coming back to this area until that day when you suggested I fill the vacancy, and now I've arrived I realise what I've been missing.'

'Fine,' his friend said. 'Come along and I'll introduce you to the staff. First the other doctors, our newlyweds Ruby and Hugo Lawrence, and then the three practice nurses. There's Helena, who has been with us for ever and is the practice's senior nurse. Then Gina, who is the mother of two young boys and works part-time to fit in with school hours. And then there is our bright morning star…'

'Oh! Not so bright this morning!' he commented as Julianne came hurrying in through the main doors of the practice looking pale and heavy-eyed, her pallor deepening when she saw Aaron standing in Reception.

As she halted on seeing them, Nathan said laughingly, 'I was just telling Aaron that you are our bright morning star, but you seem to have lost your shine today.'

'I'm sorry,' she croaked. 'I had a restless night, but I'll be all right as soon as I've had a cup of tea.' And with a grimace of a smile in Aaron's direction she added, 'Nice to meet you, Dr Somerton.'

'And you too Nurse, er…?' he replied.

'Julianne Marshall.' She waited with bated breath.

'Nice to meet you, Julianne Marshall.' And only by the flicker of an eyelid could she tell that he knew who she was.

'If you will excuse me' she said, 'I need to get changed while you are being introduced to the rest of the staff.'

Julianne scurried to the nurses' rooms, which were unoccupied at that moment.

'Ugh!' she groaned. 'That was worse than taking castor oil! I'm sure he recognised me. My name isn't one he would forget in a hurry!'

She quickly changed then headed for the kitchen.

With ten minutes before the first appointment of the day, she found Aaron in there, chatting to Laura Armitage. So purposely took her drink to the far end of the room and chatted to one of the receptionists until Nathan announced that he was about to open up, and there was a general exodus.

Their glances met briefly as Aaron stepped back to let her and the other two nurses pass, and if she'd had any doubts before as to whether he recognised her or not, the set of his mouth held the answer, and she knew that life was not going to be easy in the days to come.

Hell's bells! Aaron thought grimly as Nathan showed him his newly decorated consulting room. The dark-haired nurse was the deceitful bridesmaid who had witnessed his humiliation and been unaffected by it. What a horrendous homecoming! So much for the future being free of the past.

If he remembered rightly, at the time of the wedding that never was she'd been doing her nurse's training then, and that was about all he'd known about her, until he'd seen her composed expression when his bride had gone like a bullet from a gun.

But it was all long ago, water under the bridge. He still smarted when he thought about it, but it only happened rarely now, and it shouldn't be hard to give the '*bright morning star*' a wide berth.

Yet Nathan's next comment made that seem unlikely when he said, 'I'm thinking of pairing us doctors each with a nurse in the general day-to-day running of the practice to give a more efficient and sympathetic approach to our patients, but will wait until you've had the chance to settle in amongst us.'

'Yes, sure,' he said agreeably, but if he was 'paired' with Julianne Marshall he would wish himself back in Africa.

When Aaron went across to the bakery at lunchtime for a sandwich, the man behind the counter asked, 'Are you the new doctor?'

'Yes, I am,' he told him. 'Is there something I can help you with?'

The baker was smiling. 'Yes, you can tell Julianne, the girl who rents the apartment above the shop, that burning the midnight oil on weeknights is not a good idea for a young nurse who is on her feet all day. Maybe she'll take some notice of you.'

Aaron very much doubted it, and told the baker, 'Nurse Marshall and I have only just met. She may not welcome advice from a stranger.' The memory of hair as dark as ravens' wings swinging against bare shoulders in a shining swathe, and a red dress that had been the perfect foil for it, came to mind. He hadn't known who she was then, but felt that she must have recognised him as she'd turned her back to him in the middle of the group on the pavement when she'd seen him approaching.

Autumn was dithering on the edge of winter and the practice was busy with the inevitable flu jabs and the onset of the demand for cold medications and the age-related illnesses that flared up with the approach of the festive season, and Aaron was soon in his stride without any further sightings of Julianne Marshall since their awkward meeting in the reception area that had been followed with the cosy tea and talk time in the surgery kitchen.

But he couldn't skulk in his room all day, and why should he? On that dreadful day long ago he'd had nothing to blame himself for except maybe being too trusting, and he'd never trusted anyone completely since.

When he went into the corridor after notifying the nurses via email of certain tests he required to be done for his last patient, Julianne appeared with a printout in her hand of the instructions he'd just sent through, and as he observed her unsmilingly Aaron decided that her long legs in sheer grey tights had to be the same ones that he'd seen dashing up the back stairs in the bakery the day before.

Had she known who he was *then*? Him coming to join the practice would be general knowledge, so she would have been prepared, but to him she was someone totally unexpected who was going to be a constant reminder of a day that would haunt him for ever.

She was waiting to speak to him with dark eyes watchful and no smiles to be seen on the smooth lines of her face.

'What is it?' he asked abruptly. 'Have you got a problem with what I've just asked one of you to do?'

'No,' she said with outward calm. 'It is just that your

patient is questioning the cortisone injection in the knee that you have given him without warning.'

'Are you questioning my methods?' he said coldly. 'The man's records show that he was booked in today for that very thing. I haven't dreamt it up from somewhere. I *did* tell him what I was going to do, and now I've sent him to you for his flu and pneumonia injections *at his request*.'

'Yes, so I see,' she said meekly. 'Obviously he must have misunderstood about the injection in his knee.'

'That could be the case,' he said flatly. 'If you or he have any further doubts, I suggest you check his records for yourself.' And without giving her the chance to comment further he went to discuss the matter of where to buy a car from with Nathan, as without transport he wasn't going to be much use to the practice.

CHAPTER TWO

HE DIDN'T buy a sports car, needless to say. Instead, when he'd completed the sale he drove back to the surgery in a black four-wheel-drive, and watching him park it on the forecourt from the window of the nurse's room Julianne sighed.

Their first conversation had been a prickly affair and she couldn't visualise any future ones being any different. The only thing that would put things right between them would be for her to tell Aaron exactly what had been in her mind on that dreadful day.

It had been more of a teenage crush than a grand passion, but it hadn't seemed like that at the time, and she'd known that beside her sister's attractions her own had been almost non-existent.

Living in Nadine's shadow had become a way of life that she'd had to accept—even their parents had been known to show preference on occasion. While she'd been growing up, whenever her father had called for his beautiful daughter to come to him she'd learned never to go rushing to his side, experience having taught her that it had been Nadine he'd wanted, always Nadine.

When her sister's 'latest' had appeared on the scene, handsome, clever, a catch by anyone's standards, he had seemed like the prince to her Cinderella, and she had prayed that Nadine would not bring him grief.

In a strange sort of way her prayers had been answered. The 'grief' *had* been there, no escaping that, but to a much lesser degree than if the marriage had gone ahead, and she'd hoped with youthful optimism that Aaron might notice her with Nadine gone.

At the last moment her sister had gone where there had been money, lots of it, and Aaron had been spared the nightmare that life married to Nadine would have been, but she, Julianne, hadn't come out of it smelling of roses either.

She'd confessed to him how often she'd tried to persuade Nadine not to marry him, but in the midst of his anger hadn't been able to get the words out to tell him why, and Aaron's disgust at what he'd seen as her conniving had hit her like a sledgehammer.

When she'd left the vestry after taking time to calm herself he had disappeared and she'd never seen him again until now, when the feelings she'd had for him that had shrivelled and died over the years were seemingly springing back into life.

Aaron was out of the car and striding towards the main doors of the surgery and knowing that she would be on view she moved away from the window and found Helena, the oldest of the nurses, smiling across at her.

'So is he your type?' she asked.

'Is *who* my type?' she questioned innocently.

'Aaron Somerton. I don't doubt all of the available women will be noticing his arrival in our midst.'

'So? They will have no competition from me,' she told her. 'We knew each other in another life and didn't get on.' Turning away, she called in the first of those waiting to be seen by a nurse and it turned out to be her landlord, George, the baker, who had come for his regular B12 injection.

'The new doctor came into the shop this morning,' he said while rolling up his sleeve, 'and I asked him to impress on you that midweek living it up is not a good thing for tired nurses who have been on their feet all day.'

She was bending over him with needle poised, and hissed angrily, 'You had a nerve, George! I am quite capable of looking after myself. It is his first day with us and you say something like that to him. What was his reply?'

'Said that you'd only just met and didn't think the idea would appeal to you.'

'He got that right! It would *not* appeal to me. So will you stop fussing over me, George?'

'Aw, come on, Julianne,' he protested. 'You know you're like the daughter I never had, and I worry about you because you seem so alone. My missus is long gone so I need somebody to look after.'

She was smiling now. 'Yes, I know. But please don't talk about me to Aaron Somerton—anyone else is OK but not him.'

'All right,' he said, and in went the needle.

* * *

His first day at the practice was over and as Aaron drove back to The Falls Cottage beneath the darkening skies of an approaching winter evening the events of the day were going through his mind, and, wrongly or rightly, meeting up with Julianne Marshall, the young nondescript teenage bridesmaid of long ago and now a very attractive woman, was the one uppermost.

Her sister, blonde where Julianne was dark, had been good-looking too, otherwise she wouldn't have caught the eye of the millionaire who had been so much older than himself, and when he'd been left standing at the altar he had realised the truth of one of his mother's favourite sayings, that beauty was only skin deep.

When he and Julianne had come face-to-face in the corridor outside the nurses' room he hadn't put into words that he knew who she was. He hadn't needed to. His manner when they'd discussed the patient who'd complained about having the cortisone injection had made it clear enough. It had been while his glance had been on the printout she'd been holding that he'd seen that his surmise that she too would have found herself a husband by now had been wrong. There had been no wedding ring on her finger.

The cottage and the waterfall had come into view and as he pulled up beside them and gave the car a quick glance he thought that it was the first time he'd ever bought a car without some degree of thought, or worked his first day in a new practice with both events barely registering because of a woman, but that had been the case today,

Tomorrow was going to be different, he vowed silently. The bridesmaid of long ago was not going to put him off his stride, no way!

Later that evening Aaron went out for a stroll and ran into Helena Carey, the senior practice nurse, who was out walking her dog.

'So how did your first day go, Dr Somerton?' she asked, her frisky boxer straining at its lead.

'Fine, thank you,' he replied. 'Needless to say, it was very different from the surgeries I have worked in over the last few years, but they all have the same end in view, don't they?'

'Yes, they do,' she agreed, and then to his surprise asked, 'What do you think of the staff at the surgery?'

'They seem great. Why do you ask?'

'I thought that maybe you hadn't hit it off with Nurse Marshall as you seemed to be having a disagreement at one point during the morning. It was unusual as Julianne is held in high regard by everyone at the practice.'

'Yes, I am sure she is,' he said calmly. 'It was just a moment of confusion on both our parts, that's all.'

'Ah, that's good,' she replied, and went on her way, leaving him to think that the face from the past seemed as if she had a fan club at the surgery. So what? There would be no likelihood of him joining it. He had seen her and her sister in their true colours and was not going to be deceived twice.

That second night he slept better. The sound of the waterfall was no longer disruptive. This time it was a constant, reliable sound that helped him to relax, and no sooner had his head hit the pillow than he was out like a light.

Until he heard the sound of the first of the passenger launches going across the lake at seven o'clock the next morning and then it was a shower, a quick breakfast and off to the practice with what would have been sheer pleasure if it wasn't for the thought of meeting up again with Julianne.

As he drove along the main street she was there, brisk and immaculate, unlike her appearance of the morning before, and about to get into her car. On impulse he drew level at the kerbside and as she looked up questioningly he said tonelessly, 'I saw Helena last night down by the lake and she was concerned that we weren't going to get on with each other, so I thought I'd stop to let you know that during working hours there will be no problems as far as I am concerned, though I'm sure you must realise that if I'd known you were part of the package of Swallowbrook's health care I wouldn't have taken the job.'

Here it comes, Julianne thought miserably. *It hasn't taken him long to put me in my place. Would he have recognised me if it hadn't been for my name?* But she was not going to argue.

'I'm sorry that my presence at the surgery has taken away your pleasure in coming home, Aaron,' she said levelly. 'When I knew that you were going to be Libby's replacement, I must admit I thought about leaving, but decided that as I'd done nothing wrong, why should I?

A truce while we're working together would be most acceptable, and for the rest of the time our private lives will stay how they are meant to be, *private*.'

He didn't take her up on that, just nodded, and keen to know if she already knew that Nathan was having thoughts about them working in pairs asked, 'Did you know that Nathan is considering us working in twos, a doctor and a nurse working together?

'At the moment we have four doctors and three nurses so he will probably leave Ruby working solo until she leaves to look after their little adopted child when it arrives. It would be better if we didn't work so closely together.'

She almost groaned out loud and ignoring his last comment said, 'No, I didn't know. Maybe I can ask him not to do that before he decides who is with who, but of course he will want to know why and…'

'What? You wouldn't want him to find out that you are not as bright a star as he thinks you are? I will say one thing, Julianne, you have certainly got them all bedazzled, Nathan, Helena, the nice guy at the bakery, but of course they don't know the sort of things you get up to, do they?'

On that discordant note he drove off and left her standing on the pavement with a lump in her throat, thinking miserably that no man would relish having to endure what had happened to him, and if *she* wanted no further hurt along the way she would need to tread carefully when he was around at the practice, *which was going to be most of the time.*

When Julianne arrived Aaron was already ensconced in the kitchen with some of the other staff, enjoying the early morning brew that the first to arrive always made for the rest of them, and when he saw her downcast expression Aaron felt a sharp pang of guilt. If they'd been handing out medals for arrogance he would have been top of the list.

On impulse he said to those gathered there, 'I wonder if you folks would like to be my guests tonight at somewhere while I celebrate my return to the UK, which has brought with it the pleasure of meeting you all?'

With one exception, Julianne thought. There had been no joy for him in meeting up with her again. So what was the reason for his sudden invitation? Yet did it matter? Whatever it was, she wouldn't be attending.

For one thing, he wouldn't want her there, and for another it was her night for helping out at the hospice at the far side of the lake, and no matter how low she might be feeling she never arrived there without a smile on her face.

Nathan had just appeared and Aaron was asking him if he and Libby could get someone to mind the children for a couple of hours at such short notice.

After thinking for a moment, Nathan replied, 'I'm sure that my father will do the honours as long as both Toby and Elsey are asleep when we leave them.'

With a glance at the other two doctors, Hugo Lawrence and his recently qualified young wife, Ruby, Aaron said, 'And would you folks be free for a couple of hours?'

'Yes, of course,' Hugo replied, and to the rest of those gathered in the kitchen, 'Where would you suggest? Aaron doesn't know the night life in the area like we do. There's The Mallard, of course, or a new restaurant that has just opened on the lakeside that we've had good reports of. You have a good social life, Julianne, where do you suggest?'

'I'm not sure,' she said. 'We all have our likes and dislikes, and in any case I won't be there, it's the night I go to help out at the hospice, and I can't let them down.'

So much for that, Aaron thought. He'd suggested the get-together mainly because he felt guilty for being so abrupt earlier, and was now realising that he needn't have bothered extending an olive branch as she had other plans.

But he couldn't go back on what he'd suggested and showing no disappointment at the thought of her absence he decided on the new restaurant. A decision that was met with approval from everyone except Julianne, who was just relieved to have a good reason for not being there and didn't have to think up an excuse.

It was always very late when she arrived home on the nights she worked at the hospice. If there was an ambulance driver free, or any other member of the staff going her way with a car, they would give her a lift, otherwise she phoned for a taxi. She had a little runabout car, but was always so tired when she'd finished there after working at the practice all day that she daren't risk using it in case she fell asleep at the wheel.

Tonight it was one of the doctors at the hospice who

had brought her home and as he drove off, the surgery crowd appeared, strolling along the pavement on their way home from the impromptu party, all in high spirits after the unexpected get-together in a smart restaurant.

The last thing she wanted was to have to face Aaron again and she fumbled around in her bag for the door key, hoping to get inside before they drew level. The ones at the front didn't pause, just called their goodnights and ambled on.

At the same second that her fingers closed around the key she could see Aaron looming up in the rear, chatting to Ruby and Hugo, *and he'd seen her.*

As the other two doctors wished her goodnight he stopped beside her. She turned the key quickly in the lock and as the door swung open stepped inside then swung round to face him.

She didn't speak. If he had something to say, let him say it and be gone, she thought. *Her* evening had been spent mostly surrounded by the terminally ill with the sadness that such situations brought with them and now she just wanted to go to bed. She was tired in body and soul.

He did have something to say and it took her by surprise. 'If they are looking for volunteers at the hospice I could give them a couple of nights, or weekends, on a regular basis. Just thought I'd mention it as I was passing.' He turned to go. 'At different times to yours, of course.'

Stung by the comment, she said, 'But of course. It

wouldn't do for you to be mixing with a wrong 'un. Now, if you'll excuse me, I would like to go to bed.'

'Sure. I'll be on my way.' And without further comment he went striding off in the direction of the lake, the waterfall and the cottage, and his last thought before he slept was about Julianne again. So far she hadn't put a foot wrong. Either she was playing him up, or he'd got his wires crossed somewhere.

Maybe tomorrow he would ask her about Nadine—where she lived, how often they met and were their parents still around? Though perhaps not. He'd only been back a couple of days and was already showing an exaggerated interest in Julianne.

Both Aaron and Julianne were waiting for Nathan to mention the working-together-in-pairs arrangement and so far he hadn't, but that omission was about to be dealt with late on Friday afternoon before the surgery closed for the weekend, when he said to them, 'I've sorted out the new working arrangements.

'I will pair with Helena. Hugo with Gina, who is going to extend her hours to match his now that her young ones are capable of being left for a short time after senior school, and the two of you will make up the third pair. I have every confidence that you will work well together, with Ruby being at hand if any of us doctors are not available for some reason, until such time as she becomes a stay-at-home mother like Libby with our young ones.'

The phone in his room was ringing and before they

could say anything he'd gone to answer it. Aaron said in a low voice, 'Maybe we should let it ride if we don't want to be the objects of gossip.'

'Yes, I suppose so,' she agreed reluctantly, and without further comment went to make sure that the nurses' room was immaculate before the surgery closed for the weekend.

Nathan shortly followed her into the room.

'So you're happy with that arrangement, then, Julianne?' She shook her head.

'You're not?' he exclaimed.

'Not over the moon, no,' she said flatly. 'Do we have to?'

'Do we have to what?' he questioned, surprised at her reaction.

She was usually the easiest of people to deal with and he was taken aback by her lack of enthusiasm.

'Work together.'

'Why? Don't you like the guy?' he questioned.

'He's all right, I suppose.'

She'd once liked him a lot more than was good for her, and even now was accepting it without protest when Aaron made no secret of what *he* thought about *her*.

The head of the practice was laughing. 'Don't overdo the enthusiasm. Is there some sort of a problem that I don't know about? It isn't like you to be so choosy.'

Wanting my sister's fiancé wasn't like me either and no good came of that, she could have told him.

'Shall we see how the two of you get on together for a trial period?' he suggested.

Julianne forced a smile but said nothing more on the subject. Pulling on her coat, she wished Nathan a good weekend and headed out into the cold.

On arriving back at her cosy flat, she collapsed onto the sofa. Her usual vitality was in short supply and it was all because of what she saw as Aaron's lurking presence.

She was still stunned by his willingness to do the same as she did and offer his services to the hospice. Maybe he was lonely and needed something to fill the hours away from the surgery, but he would soon have company when it got around that the new doctor was very easy on the eye, and would be no less handsome when the tan wore off.

After she'd had a meal of sorts that evening Julianne rang the group that she usually socialised with on Friday nights and informed them that she wouldn't be going into the town to a cinema with them, as had been arranged earlier in the week, because she needed an early night after a hectic week.

It was only half-true. She'd gone with them many times when she'd been tired at the end of the week at the practice and with the time spent at the hospice and had always perked up as soon as they were all together, but those had been when Aaron hadn't been back in her life, when he'd been far away in Africa, and now it wasn't like that any more.

He was living almost near enough to touch, and although he'd made it plain that he hadn't forgotten the past and was enduring her presence at the practice only because he had no choice. She had the feeling all the time that he would be watching everything she did and wouldn't be awarding any Brownie points for excellence.

The fact remained, however, that she just couldn't stay closeted in her small apartment on a Friday night, it would be just too stifling, and on that thought she wrapped up warmly and went for a walk by the lake in the opposite direction from The Falls Cottage.

She could see in the distance that the light was on and thought that Aaron must be having a quiet night too. It was dark everywhere, the light of day having gone completely. The coloured lanterns around the lake hadn't yet come on and it was beginning to feel spooky beside the trees at the water's edge as she seemed to be the only one walking there.

With a sudden yearning for warmth and light she turned swiftly to go back the way she had come and was faced with the sound of someone moving towards her through the trees.

Bereft of her usual quick thinking, she stood motionless until a hand appeared and parted the branches of the tree nearest her at the same moment that the lanterns came on.

'What on earth are *you* doing here, rambling about on your own in the dark?' Aaron asked in gritty greeting.

She thought illogically that he would never be any good as a Father Christmas unless he had a charisma transplant.

'I'm doing the same as you, it would seem, walking by the lake,' she said calmly, 'only I'm not skulking about amongst the trees. I was just about to go back when the lights came on.'

'I don't know the place as well as you,' he told her, 'and thought I could take a short cut from one side of the lake to the other, but didn't get it quite right. I must say that you are the last person I was expecting to see out here. I would have thought Friday night would be party night.'

'It usually is in some form or other. My friends were surprised to hear that I was giving it a miss.'

'And why are you?' he asked, thinking that he must be insane, wanting to know the workings of her mind.

'I didn't want to risk meeting up with you again,' she said with a hollow laugh, 'but maybe it would have been wiser if I'd stayed in. Look at us here by the deserted lake, not a soul in sight, just the two of us. When I left the practice tonight it was with the thought that I wouldn't be seeing anything of you for two whole days, but I was wrong.'

She was hugging her top coat more tightly around her, shivering in the night air, and he said, 'Come on. I'll buy you a hot drink at the hotel and then, unwelcome as my presence might be, will see you safely home.' As she was about to refuse, he added, 'Don't argue!'

They drank their coffees largely in silence and Julianne didn't think she could feel more uncomfortable in Aaron's presence until he asked quite suddenly, 'How is it that you've never married?'

'That is soon answered,' she replied. 'The man I was attracted to didn't love me and I've never felt like that about anyone since.'

'It would seem to be that we do have one thing in common, then,' he said sombrely, and looked at his watch.

She saw him and said, 'Do you want us to make tracks?'

He shook his head and as if his thoughts were elsewhere said absently, 'Whenever you're ready will do.'

'I'm ready now,' she replied, with a sudden urge to be back where she belonged, away from this strange encounter that was the last thing she'd been expecting when she'd left the apartment earlier.

Once they were outside the bakery Julianne said, 'Thanks for the coffee, Aaron. I had no intention of breaking into your evening, just the opposite, in fact.'

'Don't fret about it,' he told her. 'It was just a one-off,' and even as he spoke he was turning in his tracks and with a wave of the hand was gone.

Unlocking the door, she began to climb the stairs and for the rest of the evening sat by the fire, wishing she hadn't had her boots on when a band had begun playing for dancing in the hotel. It would have given her the chance to test just how deep his aversion to her was.

In the days when he'd been courting Nadine and the two of them had gone out leaving her alone in the flat, she had used to pretend that she was dancing in his arms and would float around the place dreamily, *but only she knew that.*

CHAPTER THREE

It was Friday night and Julianne was drained physically and mentally by the happenings of a week that had seen Aaron back in Lakeland and herself trying to hang on to the shreds of what had been her life before that.

On any other occasion she would be out enjoying herself, but tonight wasn't just any night, it was the one when incredibly she'd spent a short time with the man she'd once thought was the answer to all her girlish dreams, and it had been an unnerving experience.

She had known from the moment of his arrival in Swallowbrook that she hadn't been forgiven for the part he thought she'd played in his moment of ghastly humiliation, yet he'd taken her for a hot drink when he'd seen her shiver in the chilly night air down by the lake, as he might do for anyone who was feeling the cold.

She sighed as she wandered listlessly around the small apartment that she had furnished with loving care when she'd first moved in after taking up the position of practice nurse at the local surgery.

Nadine's name hadn't come up once over their brief coffees. That was how she wanted it to be and prayed that he felt the same. If Aaron was prepared to accept her presence in his life again on sufferance, it would be easier to cope with than outright revulsion.

When she went to bed she turned her head into the pillow and wished that he had stayed in Africa instead of coming back to haunt her.

Back at the cottage beside the waterfall Aaron's thoughts were running along similar lines. Maybe a truce might be the best way to adjust to the coincidence of finding Julianne Marshall back in his life to such an extent. It would have been awkward enough to have her just living nearby. But the fact that she was going to be in his face all the time they were working at the surgery where his friend Nathan, who was not a man to gush, had described her as the 'bright morning star' was mind-blowing. Thank God she didn't resemble Nadine in looks. That would be the last straw. He would be packing his bags and looking for work elsewhere.

It was early, too soon to settle down for the night, and he decided to seek some company, anyone's but hers. As he walked back along the main street he saw that the lights were out in the apartment above the bakery and thought that she must have gone to meet her friends after all.

As he walked briskly along, The Mallard came into view and after a quick look around inside to make sure that Julianne and her associates weren't there, he found warmth from the wintry night and friendly chat amongst folk who some day he might find sitting across from him at the surgery.

The two Lawrence doctors, Hugo and Ruby, were seated at one of the tables with the practice manager Laura Armitage and her husband, Gabriel. When they saw him Hugo came across and invited him to join them, and putting his gloomy thoughts to one side he accepted and for the first time since his arrival in Swallowbrook started to feel as if he belonged.

As the evening progressed it was discussed that the Lawrences were expecting a child to adopt soon, which would mean that Ruby being the relief doctor in the pairing-off process might not be available for long, but there would be time enough for Nathan to sort that out when it happened.

He also discovered that Laura and Gabriel had two children—Sophie, nine years old and staying the night at a school friend's, and Josh, six, who was sleeping at Nathan's with his best friend, Toby, which had left their parents free to socialise for a change.

The conversation was mostly about themselves and the village as a whole, with frequent mentions of the practice, but as there was no reason for the nurses to come under discussion Julianne's name didn't come up and perversely Aaron wished that it would, so that he might pick up some substance regarding her life past and present with regard to the best way to cope with her unwelcome presence in his life.

As he walked back at gone midnight to where the

waterfall danced endlessly into the lake he saw that her apartment was still in darkness and thought that she was most likely still living it up somewhere. As a mini-bus unloaded a group of late-night passengers just ahead of him he quickened his step in case she was amongst them. Two accidental meetings in one night was not to be contemplated.

He would have been amazed to know that she was lying wide-eyed against the pillows in her small bedroom, with sleep hard to come by because of him, and when he arrived back at the cottage he paused for a moment before going inside.

A winter moon was turning the still, dark waters of the lake into silver, and in the background the fells, high up above, encircled it like a protective bracelet. The scene was indescribably beautiful and so was the woman who had spoiled his homecoming with her presence, but, then, *she* hadn't been exactly overjoyed to see *him* either.

All you've got to do is stick to the job and its demands when you're in her presence, he reminded himself, and for the rest of it stay out of her way. Unlocking the door of the cottage, he went slowly upstairs and tried not to dwell on how difficult that might turn out to be.

With Friday gone, Saturday dawned bright and cold, and when Julianne awoke after falling asleep in the early hours with the short time she'd spent with Aaron the last thing on her mind, it was also the first when she opened her eyes, and she groaned softly.

She'd been content before he had reappeared on the scene, happy and fulfilled in her job, safe in the home she had made for herself above George's bakery, where he liked to feel he was keeping a fatherly eye on her. There was no need, of course, but it gave him pleasure to do so and she was happy to go along with it as she saw little enough of her own father.

After the fiasco of her sister's wedding day she had kept free of any romantic entanglements, only dating casually.

Since Aaron had disappeared from her life she had never really cared for any other man because he had been so much what she longed for, but he had been swift to think badly of her when all she had done had been to try to save him hurt. Now, amazingly, he had come back into her life after a long absence and she wasn't going to make that mistake again.

She usually helped George in the shop downstairs on Saturday mornings by serving the customers, and after the bakery was closed went into the town to shop and have an evening meal in one of the restaurants there.

Today was going to be no different, she decided with the lie-in she'd promised herself taking a back seat. After a hasty breakfast she went down to the shop to help George as customers came and went after buying the bread and cakes that he had baked during the dawn hours, and it was only when Aaron appeared amongst those waiting to be served that she thought again how very different it was going to be having him around, and around he was going to be for the foreseeable future. So she could either get used to the idea or look for another job, and why should she have to do that? He was the intruder, not her.

He was observing her thoughtfully as he waited to be served. The dark mass of her hair was tied back neatly and she was wearing a crisp white apron over jeans and a sweatshirt.

As she served the village folk Julianne chatted easily to each customer, mainly because she knew most of them, until it was his turn and then she clammed up, was civil but not forthcoming, and he knew she was regretting the brief time they'd spent together the night before.

Yet if she was, she had a nerve. He was the one with good reason not to want to spend time with *her*, *and* coming to the bakery for bread and pastries had nothing to do with her being there. It was the excellence of the food that had brought him to the shop and he had to eat, for heaven's sake!

But as he walked back the way he'd come he knew that he could have bought the food he required at one of the other shops. It might not have been as appetising, but the bakery wasn't the only place that supplied that kind of commodity. It was a matter of him having seen what George had to offer his customers that had brought them face-to-face again.

He had the rest of the day planned. In the afternoon he intended to hire a boat, sail the full length of the lake and maybe have dinner at a restaurant at the moorings at the far end. It would be a solitary way to spend the time, but that wouldn't bother him as for the last five years spent in an overcrowded African hospital solitude had been in short supply.

Fortunately it had been the last thing he'd craved when he'd first gone out there. Time to think would have brought reminders of something he had been desperate to forget.

When Julianne came down from her apartment dressed for her weekly visit to the town George was tidying up before closing and said teasingly, 'You weren't very chatty with the new doctor again. What's the problem, has he got a wife and half a dozen offspring?'

'Not that I know of,' she told him, 'unless he's got them hidden away in Africa, and as to my not falling over myself to be nice to him, I don't have to gush over every customer who comes in, do I?'

'No,' he said, 'but you were the only woman in the place who didn't cast an eye in his direction.'

'Yes, well, that may be,' she told him, 'but when I cast an eye it won't be in Aaron Somerton's direction.' And before George could question her further she planted a kiss on his cheek and seconds later drove off in the direction of the motorway that ran past the village.

As she wandered around the shops Julianne thought that what she'd said to George had sounded convincing, so why did she have a sudden yearning to have her hair cut and styled, her nails manicured, and didn't think twice about buying a dress that she'd hesitated over for weeks because of the price?

'Please don't let me start wanting Aaron again,' she begged the unseen fates. 'It hurt too much last time and it will be the same now if I let my heart rule my head.'

As he sailed across the lake on a chilly November afternoon Aaron saw a solitary house on an island and wondered who was fortunate enough to live there.

He didn't remember it from when he'd lived not far away himself, and would surely recall it if it had been already there then. As he sailed nearer he had his answer. Nathan, Libby and their children had just disembarked from what must be their own craft and were waving to him from a small landing stage, and as he hailed them in return he felt a sharp twinge of envy.

Like the Armitages and the Lawrences, the Gallaghers had their lives sorted, it seemed. He was of a similar age to Nathan and his was far from having any stability in it because of the fickleness of a woman he should not have had anything to do with in the first place...and the same applied to her sister to a lesser degree.

He didn't linger at the moorings to dine. The light was fading, there were rainclouds above, and he wanted to get the boat back to where he'd hired it from before darkness fell. Maybe he would venture onto the lake again soon, but the next time he would like it to be in a small craft of his own.

As he was leaving the boatyard to walk home to The

Falls Cottage the rain came, heavy and drenching. He quickened his steps and halted almost in the same instant as a pink car pulled up alongside him. When he bent to look inside its small interior Julianne Marshall said, 'Can I give you a lift?'

His first thought was that he would rather get wet, and the second was that it would be churlish to refuse the offer, so he said. 'Er, yes, thank you very much,' and eased into the seat beside her.

Into the silence that followed he said, 'I've been having my first taste of sailing on the lake and enjoyed it immensely, but when you stopped beside me I was wishing that I'd gone to the boatyard in my car.'

She nodded and informed him, 'I've been into the town, shopping, which is my regular Saturday treat.'

'Good for you,' he said, and then he couldn't help himself. He had to know. 'How is Nadine these days?'

He watched her grip tighten on the steering wheel but her voice was level enough as she replied, 'All right, I would imagine. We're not in touch.'

'Really? I always thought you were close.'

'Yes, I know you did, but you were wrong.'

The Falls Cottage had come into view. In a few seconds he would be gone and Julianne thought desperately that she was being given an opportunity to tell him the true circumstances of the part she had played in his humiliation.

But would he believe her, and could she stand the embarrassment of having to explain that she'd longed for him to be hers at that time? It might make him think that she still had yearnings for him and that really would make him want to give her a wide berth.

As she watched Aaron unfold himself out of the car she let the opportunity pass. A hurried conversation about something so important and personal was not the way to put things right between them. It needed the right time and the right place and as she drove off with a farewell wave of the hand it seemed unlikely *that* was going to happen.

On the way home she felt weepy and sad. She had wished that she could have been the bride on that dreadful day, eager to make him happy and contented, and if that had been so they might have had children by now, young ones to cherish and take delight in. But instead her love for him had grown cold, just as cold as Aaron's manner towards her, so what was there left to dream about?

George was out when she arrived back at the bakery. He always took his lady friend out on Saturdays when the shop was closed for the weekend, and Julianne was relieved. If he saw her all downcast and weepy he would want to know what was wrong, and there was no way she would want to tell him.

She and her friends always congregated in the pub on Saturdays and they would be expecting her to join them there, so she supposed that she might as well. Moping around the apartment was all right for one night but it could get to be a habit if she let it, and if Aaron's presence in the village was going to be a permanent thing she was going to have to accept it and not let it assume the sort of proportions that were going to disrupt the happy life she'd made for herself here.

When she arrived at The Mallard it was later than usual and a cheer went up from the friends who had saved her a place at a corner table where they had settled themselves. When she joined them it felt better to be back in routine, doing the things she normally did, instead of letting Aaron's presence throw her off course.

The feeling was short-lived. Bright-eyed and happy, she was describing to her friend Anna the dress she'd bought when the door opened and into the warmth of a big log fire came Aaron.

As he approached the bar he nodded briefly and she responded with a weak smile. The Mallard was the centre of everyone's entertainment on winter nights like this, and it stood to sense that someone as alone as Aaron would be drawn to it.

'That's the new doctor who has just come in, isn't it?' Anna said, her attention diverted from the description of the dress. 'He is stunning, but doesn't smile much. Is he married?'

It was a casual question on her friend's part, but it brought back memories that were far from that. First and foremost was Aaron's ashen face as he'd watched her sister turn and run away from him. Flying down the aisle to where the man with the money waited in the flashy red car that had been speeding out of sight by the time her bridegroom had gathered his wits and chased after her.

'Aaron isn't married, as far as I know. He seems to be very much alone.'

Knowing that Anna was engaged to Tom, seated next to her, and that the two of them were madly in love, she teased, 'Why do you want to know? You haven't fallen out of love with Tommy, have you?'

'No. I will never do that,' she said softly. 'I was thinking of you when I asked if the dishy doctor was married.'

'Yes, well, don't,' Julianne told her. 'I am the last person Aaron Somerton would ever want to get to know better.' And having no intention of ever telling anyone about how she came to know him, she watched in silence as he went to sit at an empty table at the opposite end of the room.

He might have known that the 'bright morning star' would be shining somewhere in Swallowbrook on a Saturday night, but there was no point in fretting about that as their paths were going to be crossing all the time.

When he looked up their glances locked, hers solemn, his pleasant enough, and when he raised his glass to her he saw the colour rise in her cheeks and the next moment she was on her feet and coming across to where he was seated, and it seemed as if she was out to surprise him.

'Would you like to join us, Aaron?' she said awkwardly. 'My friends are a nice lot and would enjoy meeting you.'

The dark violet eyes looking into his were apprehensive, as if she'd overstepped the mark by inviting him to join them, and he said, improvising quickly, 'I would like to, Julianne, but I'm afraid that I must refuse. I only came in here briefly and must go in the next couple of minutes. I'm expecting a phone call from one of my colleagues in Africa and she will be disappointed if I'm not there when she rings.'

He was getting to his feet, already about to leave, and she wondered if what he'd just said was true, or if it was something he'd concocted to provide a reason not to be in her company.

Halting briefly, anxious to change the subject, he said, 'What do you folks do on Sundays in this place? Where I've been it was just like any other day.'

'I help at the hospice, if you remember me telling you, on a weeknight and on Sundays for six hours. It is only a couple of miles away and when I've finished there I do my chores,' she told.

'Ah, yes, I remember,' he said. 'I told you to tell them that I would be willing to volunteer my services if they wanted them, didn't I? Now, I really must be going or I'll miss my phone call. I will see you on Monday, no doubt.' And with a wave of the hand in the direction of those she'd left to come over to talk to him he went striding off into the night.

The excuse he'd come up with to prevent him joining Julianne and her friends had been partly true. He *was* expecting a phone call from elderly Margaret Willoughby, who he had worked alongside in Africa, but it wasn't as imminent as he'd made out.

It was an arrangement they'd made before he'd left

there that she would ring him tonight to hear how he was experiencing being back on his own territory, but it would be at least an hour before the call came through.

He wasn't happy with himself at the way he'd refused Julianne's invitation, but he'd already seen her earlier when she stopped to give him a lift in the heavy downpour and that was as far as he'd wanted it to go.

But, no, she'd been in his sights again in The Mallard, and it was going to continue, the constant being in each other's company. More so at the practice, which he was adjusting to, but also socially, and he wasn't happy about that for one good reason.

The hurts of what had happened at the church that day were long gone. He had wiped out of his mind the humiliation of it, and having no desire to be twice bitten had not been involved in any relationships with women since.

And then along had come the sister of his jilting bride and he'd been dumbstruck to find her living and working in the place he had come home to. It had brought back memories that he could certainly do without.

He knew if he had met Julianne under any other circumstances as the person she was now he would have been attracted to her, but never as one of the unholy sisters with a little smile tugging at the corners of her mouth on his wedding day, whatever she might appear to be now there would always be the reminder of that every time he saw her.

The phone call that he was expecting came through at the appointed time and afterwards, resisting the urge to go back to The Mallard and make up for his ungracious behaviour of earlier, he took a book up to bed and after leafing through it with little interest lay back against the pillows and decided to call it a day.

It was much later when Julianne decided to do the same. They had all stayed at The Mallard until past midnight and then had gone to eat at a nearby restaurant where they usually ended up on Saturday nights.

For the first time ever she hadn't enjoyed any part of the evening and it was all because of Aaron, who, it would seem, was still critical of her, wary as if she wasn't to be trusted, and after his glib excuse for not joining her and her friends she had felt the sting of rebuff below the surface.

She worked at the hospice from ten until four on Sundays and after another restless night almost overslept, but a quick shower and an even more hasty breakfast found her setting off on time on a morning that was cold, clear and frosty.

As she drove along the road that ran by the lake Aaron's reminder that he would be willing to do the same kind of voluntary work was foremost in her thoughts. Would he follow the suggestion through? she wondered. If he did it would be another day of the week when they would be in each other's company, another day of awkwardness and stress that she could do without.

But there were patients in the calm and caring atmosphere of the hospice who would benefit from his skills and competence, and who was she to want to deny them that?

When she appeared on the ward where she always worked her eyes widened and her heartbeat quickened. Not only had Aaron followed through his suggestion, he was there before her, being shown around the place by the one of the hospital's management team.

As she goggled at him he said smoothly, 'Good morning, Nurse Marshall,' and to his companion who was observing him in some surprise, 'We both work at the Swallowbrook Medical Practice and it was Nurse Marshall who put the idea into my head of offering my services to the hospice.'

The other man, smart-suited and fiftyish, said with a smile, 'Well done, Nurse. Our patients look forward to Nurse Marshall appearing beside their beds on Sundays.'

Still goggling, Julianne flashed him a weak smile in return and said, 'If that is the case I had better not disappoint them.' And leaving them to their tour of the hospice she went to do what she was there for.

As he watched her go Aaron thought that he could have at least warned her of his intention, but as the idea to go and have a look round the hospice had only occurred to him in the moment of waking it would have been an imposition to disturb her at that hour, and when the curtains of the apartment had still been closed when he'd gone to get a newspaper at the village store, he had gone without informing her of his intention.

The urge that had brought him there so soon after

mentioning it the previous night had come from his reluctance to join her and her friends when he'd been invited, and the idea of meeting up with her at the place where he knew he would find her had been a sort of olive branch, a chance to let her see that he wasn't as averse to her company as he was making out.

He wasn't intending to stay long as his joining the staff in the role of a volunteer doctor would have to be sanctioned by the authorities, but at least he had let Julianne see that he had accepted her presence in his life.

He could easily have conveniently forgotten his suggestion that he also would be willing to help at the hospice, but instead he had acted on it immediately to show her that he wasn't as keen to avoid her as she might think.

CHAPTER FOUR

As Julianne performed her duties for the terminally
ill with the ready smile and gentle nursing that was the
way of the hospice she put Aaron's unexpected appearance to the back of her mind. It would be time enough
to think about that when she was home in the silence
of the apartment.

Back at The Falls Cottage, he was doing the opposite, reliving the moment when she'd appeared on the
ward and found him already there.

Once the management had checked him out, what
might have been a future of empty Sundays would soon
be filled with caring for the sick.

If she was willing to give up part of her weekends,
so was he, and there was nothing to indicate that they
would be working together as it was a large complex.

As she drove home in the late winter afternoon Julianne was thinking about when she'd first met him.
She'd been used to Nadine always having a man in her
life. None of them lasted very long, but her sister wasn't
happy unless she was admired and lusted after.

They had come and gone, and until the night that

Aaron Somerton had appeared, Julianne hadn't taken much notice of any of them, but he had been different, so different it had taken her breath away.

With their parents never around, she and Nadine had been sharing a flat in the town centre and the arrangements had been that when she had a new man in her life her young sister had to keep out of the way, which hadn't usually been any hardship.

But with Aaron it had been attraction at first sight for her. She'd felt weak and breathless at the sight of him. His attractions had been many, as had been her sister's, and at nineteen and of average appearance she had wanted to run away and hide from them both.

He had been tall and athletic with thickly waving russet hair and hazel eyes in a face that had become fixed in her mind from the first moment of seeing him, and for some inexplicable reason he had been attracted to her mercenary sister.

She had never been attracted to anyone since because no man had ever had the appeal that he'd had for her, and though those feelings were long dead, and his coming back into her life was by accident rather than by design, it had brought a glimmer of joy that she was going to have to ignore if she didn't want it to become the aching longing of before.

Monday morning came all too soon and it was hectic after a weekend of awkward meetings that hadn't brought much pleasure for either of them.

Patients were still attending to have flu vaccinations as well as make the usual day-to-day demands of the practice nurses, and Helena was missing. She'd had a fall while out walking her dog over the weekend and had twisted her ankle badly, so it was all systems go in their part of the surgery.

Aaron was aware of the pressure that Julianne was under and was impressed with the calm composure she was displaying in the circumstances. Apart from a brief greeting on arrival they hadn't spoken, so there was no way that he knew what she'd thought of his unexpected appearance at the hospice.

Whatever it was, it wouldn't be much to his credit, he'd thought as he'd driven past the bakery on his way to the practice. It was she who had given him the idea of voluntary work and he'd acted on it without the courtesy of informing her of what he was intending.

Totally out of nowhere had come the wish that her appeal wasn't so heart-stopping, that the sister in the shadows of five years ago had stayed there after letting him see whose side *she* was on.

Yet when he'd asked after Nadine she had made it clear that they didn't communicate, being quick to point out that they had never been as close as *he'd* thought they were.

When he'd met up with her soon after his arrival in the village he'd thought that Julianne had certainly come out of her shell, that she'd appeared to be just as pleasure-loving and wanting to be seen as the woman who had turned him into a permanently single guy, but he'd been wrong.

The nurse, crisply efficient, who was coping with

the large Monday morning influx of the population of Swallowbrook was nothing like that in reality. It was no use denying it any more. If she'd been anyone else but Julianne he would want to be with her every possible moment instead of keeping her at a distance.

Ruby, Hugo's young wife, had noted the pressure that the two nurses were under and was helping every time she wasn't in consultation with a patient. If she hadn't been able to assist he would have offered his own assistance.

But the smile that Julianne had flashed at Ruby when she'd appeared would have made any welcoming of *his* assistance seem pale by comparison.

He wanted to talk to her, laugh with her, flirt with her, he was so aware of her, but Julianne wasn't just anyone, she had seen him brought low when he should have been on a high and had appeared to be happy rather than appalled by it.

When he had seen all his own patients he went to the nurses' room and found her taking blood from a woman in her late fifties for ESR testing to check for inflammation of the muscles, and when she had finished he asked, 'I'm going across to the bakery for a sandwich, can I get either of you anything while I'm there?'

'Yes, please,' she said gratefully. 'We're going to have to work through the lunch hour and I'm already famished as I didn't have breakfast this morning.'

'Why was that?' he asked in a low voice out of the patient's hearing.

She stared at him in surprise. Was he really interested in why she'd skipped breakfast? She wasn't used to anyone being concerned about her well-being to that extent and said flippantly, 'I had a restless night and then slipped into a sound sleep when I shouldn't have.'

'Ah, I see,' he said, without further comment about her working so hard on an empty stomach, and followed it by, 'So what do you want me to get for you at the bakery?'

'A sandwich and a pastry, please. If you tell George that it's for me, he knows what I like.'

With a glance at the communicating door between the two nurse's rooms he wanted to know, 'And what does Gina usually have for lunch?'

'She brings it with her. Gina is better organised than I am when it comes to food, probably because she has a young family and there are always hungry mouths waiting to be fed.'

Was there envy in her voice? he wondered. If her parenting skills were anything like her nursing ones, she would make a lovely mother, but for some reason that must be a road she wasn't yet ready to travel along. Freedom must have the greater appeal.

The amiable George knew exactly what she liked to eat and Aaron felt a twinge of irritation at what he saw as his smug hold over her. But it disappeared quickly when the baker said, 'Julianne has parents that she never sees and a sister that she once told me left a fantastic guy at the altar because some old moneybags was beckoning. So much for family life, eh?'

Yes, indeed, Aaron thought as he made his way back to the practice. So much for the *fantastic* guy that she'd told George about. The description didn't fit in with what she'd said to him in the vestry.

Back at the surgery the nurses were still busy and, appearing briefly, he told her, 'The food is on the table in the surgery kitchen.'

She flashed him a smile and said with gentle mockery, 'You are so kind, Dr Somerton.'

'Don't overdo the meekness, it doesn't suit you,' he said dryly. 'I recollect you more as a behind-the-scenes manipulator.'

'Do you?' she flared when the patient she'd just been attending had gone. 'And I remember you as the bully who dragged me into the vestry to be given the third degree and passed judgement on me without giving me any chance to explain!'

Wow! There was a world of hurt in what she'd just said. He'd been under the impression that he had been the only one to suffer from what Nadine had done to him. What did Julianne mean? Yes, he *had* questioned her angrily that day *and* with cool cheek she'd told him that she'd been in the background, trying to persuade her sister to call off the wedding.

He'd never got around to asking her why. It had been the last straw. He'd slammed out of the church and out of her life, and now he was back in it and she was back in his, and it was turning the homecoming he had so looked forward to into a maze of confused feelings.

Julianne had patients outside in the corridor, who

were watching the clock. It was not the moment for this sort of discussion. 'Maybe another time you will explain what you meant by that,' he said, and left her wishing that she hadn't brought painful memories back at such a moment, or at any moment for that matter. With a smile that was not as bright as before she called in the next patient.

When she found a few moments in the quietness of the surgery staffroom to eat the food that Aaron had brought, Nathan came seeking her out and said, 'Helena hopes to be back with us tomorrow, Julianne. I'm sorry that today has been so hectic. If for any reason she doesn't make it, I'll get a bank nurse to come and help out. OK?'

She nodded, and observing her thoughtfully he asked, 'Is everything all right with you? You haven't seemed your usual happy self of late, which seems to coincide with Aaron joining us. Are you and he getting on all right?'

'Yes, we're fine,' she told him, perking up for his benefit. It was obvious that Nathan didn't know they'd met before and under what circumstances, and there was no way she was going to embarrass Aaron by mentioning to anyone what had happened to him on what must have been one of the worst days of his life. Her part in it of a devastated onlooker had been bad enough, but for him it must have been appalling.

Over the years she'd convinced herself that her feelings for him then had been the youthful crush of a nineteen-year-old girl for a man a few years older who had been the personification of her dream man. Yet why did her heart beat faster and her legs still turn to jelly whenever he was near?

'That's good,' Nathan said, adding on the point of departing, 'Did you know that he's an expert on tropical diseases? I wouldn't be surprised if his stay with us is short and he moves on to a consultant's position somewhere abroad again.'

When he'd gone she sat gazing into space with the food untouched. She'd lost her appetite. What Nathan had just said had wiped out all her determination not to fall in love with Aaron again because nothing had changed, her feelings for him had been just put on hold for the last five years.

She'd convinced herself that they were dead and they weren't. If he was going to be here today and gone tomorrow she wouldn't be able to bear it, and her being around constantly might make him feel that the sooner he was gone the better.

At the end of the day she decided to walk home, leaving her car at the practice overnight. She was tired, it had been a busy day, but there were always those and she took them in her stride.

It had been dark since four o'clock and there was the nip of frost in the air, yet she felt as if she couldn't breathe, felt weak and listless, and that maybe the short walk home would liven her up and bring back her confidence, because it was as if there was nowhere to go, nowhere to hide from the revelation of her true feelings for the man who'd call her a manipulator.

When his car stopped beside her she felt no surprise. Aaron would have to take the same direction as she was taking to get to The Falls Cottage. He wound the window down and his first words were, 'What's the matter with your car? Wouldn't it start?'

'That isn't the reason why I'm on foot,' she told him. 'I felt that I needed some air to clear my head of all the happenings of the day.'

'Any happening in particular?' he wanted to know. 'And are you going to get in and let me drive you the rest of the way? I'm going to eat out tonight instead of cooking. Do you want to come along?'

He'd just rattled off three questions, all tricky to answer, and she answered the second one by seating herself in the passenger seat next to him. With regard to the first there was no reply forthcoming, and for the last she looked down at the dark blue nurse's dress that she'd worn at the surgery and instead of telling him she would love to have a meal set in front of her that someone else had prepared said, 'I'm hardly dressed for dining out, but thanks just the same.'

'I can wait while you go home to change,' he offered, wondering if he was going insane. He should be avoiding Julianne, not actively finding ways to spend more time in her company!

If he was acting out of character, so was she. 'Yes, all right,' she agreed. 'If you come up to the apartment you can have a coffee while I shower and change.'

'What about George, your protector?' he asked half-jokingly. 'Won't he want to check me over first?'

He watched her colour rise but her reply was casual enough as she told him, 'The bakery is closed. George lives in the house next door and at this moment will be having his meal in front of the television.'

'So you are in this huge place on your own during the night?' he said as they climbed the stairs to the apartment.

'Er, yes, I suppose you could say that.'

'Do I take it that there is a fire escape?'

'Yes, it's round the back.'

'Good, I'm glad to hear it.'

He was visualising The Falls Cottage, cosy and compact, easily entered and left, and comparing it with this place on the top of large shop premises that contained big ovens.

When she unlocked the door and they went in he saw that her home was nicely decorated in restful colours with polished wooden floors, attractive scatter rugs and tasteful furniture around the place, and not a photograph in sight, which was odd.

Julianne appeared at that moment with coffee and biscuits and said, 'I won't be long, Aaron. You could have been already eating if you hadn't stopped for me.'

He was smiling. 'There is no rush as far as I'm concerned. We have the whole evening ahead of us, and as you are much more knowledgeable than I am with regard to Swallowbrook and its surroundings maybe you would like to choose where we eat. And why don't you have a coffee before you go to get ready? Like I said, there is no rush, not unless you are gasping for food.'

'I'm ravenous,' she replied, 'but the coffee will keep the hunger pangs at bay for a while and then I really will go and shower away the germs of a busy day at the practice. Did you ever pick up anything infectious while you were in Africa?'

'No. I suppose one gets immune to a lot of diseases by being constantly amongst them. I had been out there just a year when Nathan arrived on a three-year contract and we became good friends. When he came home at the end of it I still had twelve months to do and getting to know him set me off wanting to come back to the UK. And as you see, here I am.'

'To stay?' The words were out before she could stop them and his reply came just as fast.

'Why? Does it matter?'

'No, of course not. I'm just curious, that's all.'

He didn't believe her. She wanted him gone. He was a reminder of the past, of a time when she had plotted against him and felt his anger.

She'd been perched on a stool near the fire, warming her hands around the coffee cup, but now she was on her feet, moving towards the bedroom and telling him as if they had talked enough, 'I won't be long.'

'Sure,' he said easily, and as if there'd been no un-comfortable vibes between them picked up a magazine from a table beside him and began to glance through it.

Julianne was quick in the shower but not so fast in choosing what to wear. She had an insane urge to dress up for him, to wear something striking, but they were merely going for a bite to eat at the end of their working day so it didn't call for trying to impress.

Eventually she reappeared in a black miniskirt with leggings and high boots and a chunky white sweater and waited for his reaction, which was disappointing when it came.

'You'll need a top coat,' he commented. 'It's going to be a very cold night according to the weather forecast.'

There was no warmth in his glance as he observed her and she wondered what she had expected. He was probably wishing he hadn't been so ready with the invitation to join him and was taken aback that she'd been so quick to accept it.

As she went to do as he'd suggested and came back with a cosy furry jacket, it was in her mind that because she was facing up to the fact that she'd never really stopped loving him, it didn't mean that Aaron was any happier with her now than he'd been all that time ago.

There was silence between them as they left the apartment and the sound of their feet on the wooden staircase that led to ground floor level echoed eerily in the stillness.

Aaron was thinking that Julianne must think him a prize fusspot. Fussing about her lunch when it seemed as if she wouldn't have time to go to the bakery. Driving her home when she would probably have preferred to walk, and last but not least suggesting that she was being foolish if she went out into the winter night without a coat.

When she'd appeared ready to leave with her hair swept up in a shining coil and the blue nurse's dress discarded in favour of more fashionable clothes, he had been so stunned by the feelings she'd aroused in him that he'd concealed it by commenting about her not wearing a coat. So no doubt she was wondering why he was so concerned about her well-being when he didn't even like her.

He was wrong. A kind word from the man by her side was a precious thing and she prayed that one day he might freely forgive her for the wrong that he thought she had done him.

On the surface pleasure-loving and bright, she had always known what it was like to feel alone, even when she'd been young, because she had always been passed over by her parents in favour of Nadine, and then in recent years when they had begun to do their own thing, with her mother remarrying and her father sailing the seas non-stop, she had ended up sharing a flat with her sister and the loneliness had persisted as Nadine had ignored her most of the time.

Once she had gone to be with her lover it had been a matter of leaving the flat and moving to Swallowbrook when she'd got the job at the surgery, and from then on she'd been able to live her life how she wanted and might have found some degree of contentment if only she had been able to put matters right with Aaron before he'd disappeared, so now in this time of second chances, a kind word from him was something to treasure.

In a less kind moment since he had come back into

her life he had called her a manipulator and it had hurt. If she had been that, she would have thought of some way of stopping the wedding, but at nineteen and facing the kind of threat that Nadine had held over her, she hadn't known which way to turn.

If it had been now, when she was more mature and confident, everything would have been different.

'So where do you suggest we eat?' he asked.

'How about The Falls Bistro?' she suggested. 'It's a new place about a mile past your cottage and the food is good.'

He nodded. 'Yes, sounds OK. Let's go.'

When they passed the cottage with the waterfall tumbling beside it she asked, 'How do you like living there?'

'It's great' was the reply. 'It's so comfortable and nicely furnished, and being able to see the lake all the time is fantastic. My first night I didn't settle well because the noise of the water kept me awake, but I soon adjusted. The endlessness of it is rather comforting as there are so many things in life that don't last. Apart from the waterfall everywhere else is wonderfully silent until the first of the passenger launches comes sailing past at seven o'clock.'

'What do you think of where I live?' she wanted to know, having taken note of his question about a fire escape.

'Your apartment is tasteful and spacious' was his reply, followed by silence.

'But?' she prompted.

'You *are* all alone up there when the bakery is closed.'

'Yes, I know,' she agreed, 'but the place is fitted out with fire and burglar alarms…and I'm used to being on my own.'

'Where are your parents these days? Are they still not around?'

'No, my mother lives in Australia with her new husband and my father is still sailing the ocean as steward on a yacht that belongs to an American couple. So nothing has changed as far as they are concerned. We never were a close family.'

'And is that how you want it to be?' he questioned as the lights of the bistro came into view.

'Absolutely not!' she exclaimed. 'If I ever have any children I will want them to have all the things that I've missed. What about you? I never knew much about you. When Nadine began bringing you to the flat I was always ordered to stay out of the way. Do you have family? I don't remember them at the wedding.'

There! She'd said it! The 'wedding' word and the earth hadn't moved or the seas begun to swell.

'My parents died while I was at college and I was an only child, so I had no family present on that day, thank God! Life was not always a bundle of joy having no brothers or sisters to play with when I was young and I always said that when I married I would have a house full of children, but it turned out that your sister had other plans and since then I haven't taken any chances.'

She couldn't believe what was happening. They

were actually talking about it. The barriers were coming down, but what difference would it make to her side of it? She couldn't tell Aaron that he'd been her dream man at that time. He had barely known she'd existed and would be bound to find the telling of it an exercise in bad taste.

The car park of the bistro was almost empty, Monday night wasn't a popular night for eating out, and the frost and ice everywhere was thickening, so much so that when she swung her legs out of the car and stood upright on the tarmac she felt herself slipping and Aaron, who had just come round from the driver's side, reached out and caught her before she fell.

When she looked up at him from the protective circle of his arms it was as if she belonged there. He was holding her for the first time ever, not flesh to flesh, more thick winter coat against thick winter coat, but it was where she wanted to be, and as he looked down at her beneath the cold, starlit sky, for the first time in years desire was warming his blood.

He didn't want it to, especially remembering who she was, but it was there, the heat of it, and with eyes pleading and colour deepening, Julianne reached up and kissed him on the lips. It was just a fleeting gesture but its effect was far from light.

He swung her off her feet and kissed her in return and it went on and on until she pushed him away, gasping for breath, and he came to his senses, unable to believe that he had let his guard down with the same family that had once humiliated him big time.

'I'm sorry,' he told her brusquely. 'I shouldn't have let you take the initiative. I know your family all too well.' He turned towards the brightly lit bistro. 'We've come here to eat, that's all. Shall we go and do just that?'

She nodded and without speaking followed meekly as he led the way into the warmth that awaited them.

The food was good as she had said it would be, but as far as Julianne was concerned it tasted of nothing, because her mouth was still warm from his kisses and the rest of her was aching for more, but in her heart there was dismay.

She'd been too eager, too desperate to stay in Aaron's arms, and the delicate process of getting to know each other better had been blown away.

He had referred to her family with a degree of bitterness that had shown he hadn't either forgiven or forgotten the past and the moment they had finished eating they were both ready to leave, wanting to put what had happened in the car park out of their minds, and knowing *that* wasn't going to happen.

There was silence between them until Aaron stopped the car in front of the bakery and said levelly, 'I can't help feeling that any attraction between us would be lunacy. Maybe I should move on somewhere else. I would never have come to Swallowbrook if I'd known that I was going to find you here.'

'Is that so?' she said tightly, as he demolished her dreams with just a few cutting words. 'Maybe some time I might tell you exactly what my part was in what happened to you that day in the church.' And before he could reply she was gone, slamming the door behind her, and as the lock clicked into position she walked slowly up the staircase to the sanctuary that she had made for herself.

CHAPTER FIVE

So much for Aaron ever loving me for myself, let alone liking me, Julianne thought miserably as she lay sleepless through the night hours. He had condemned her because of her family who, she admitted, were not perfect, but they were all she had.

The moments in his arms had been magical, as if there might be a chance for them. She'd dared to hope, and should have known better. In a sad sort of way she supposed he had done her a favour by voicing his regret for what had happened between them. It was better than pretending. He had talked of moving on to another position to get away from the embarrassment of her presence and if he did that she would feel desolate. Yet if they were never going to be able to put the past to rest, what other answer was there?

Aaron stood looking out into the night, watching the water cascade into the lake and thinking that those moments in the car park of the bistro had come from a force that had a similar impetus, sweeping every other thing out of its way with the power of the attraction between them, and when he had come up for air, what had he done? He'd treated Julianne as if she was someone to be avoided, a threat to his existence, when it was time that he stopped feeling sorry for himself.

Raking his hands through the russet thatch of his hair, he groaned at the thought of his arrogance towards her. They would be in close contact at the surgery tomorrow and he would apologise at the first opportunity that presented itself, but private moments between staff were not always possible once the busy day got under way.

His thoughts turned to Gabriel Armitage, the oncologist who had been headhunted to be in charge of the new cancer clinic next to the surgery. He was happily married to Laura, the practice manager, who seemed to have no problem with the fact that he had just served a prison term for attacking a man who had been behaving offensively towards her, and yet he, Aaron, all high and mighty, was treating Julianne as if she was guilty of far worse than that.

He drew the curtains across impatiently to shut out the waterfall and went up to bed, and his last thought before falling into a restless sleep was the apology he owed the woman who had melted in his arms. Where all the passion had come from he didn't know, but knew if it happened again he would be lost in the wonder of it.

It was as he thought it might be the next morning. The doctors were busy with the first lot of patients of the day, and the nurses were coping with the ones that were being passed on to them for blood tests, flu jabs and fresh dressings on injuries sustained in one way and another, which was keeping them all busily occupied.

Helena was back but leaning on a stick to take the pressure off her foot, and it was slowing down her usual brisk approach to whatever came the way of the three nurses during surgery hours. So Julianne was once again taking on the responsibility for the efficient functioning of the nursing side of the practice and glad of it, as it was keeping Aaron at a distance with regard to everything except the patients.

By the middle of the afternoon the busiest part of the day was over and he went to seek her out in the nurse's room but was taken aback when Helena said, 'Dr Gallagher has sent Julianne home. Nathan thinks she might be sickening for something and insisted that she go home to rest.'

It was more likely that she was 'sickened' rather than 'sickening', he thought bleakly as he went back to his own room. The opportunity to say he was sorry was slipping out of his grasp unless he stopped off at her apartment on his way home in the early evening.

When he arrived at the bakery George was on the point of closing for the night and Aaron said, 'I just want a quick word with Julianne. Is she available?'

'I think not' was the reply. 'When she came home our girl said she didn't want any visitors. It seems to me that they might be working her too hard at that surgery.'

As he prepared to drive off Aaron thought that she wasn't taking any chances that he might get to her. The 'no visitors' comment would be for his ears only, which left just the choice of a phone call to make his apology and he would wait until he was back at the cottage before he did that.

When there was no answer he put a ready meal in the oven and went to change out of the clothes he'd worn for the surgery. An hour later he pushed the plate away with the food half-eaten and reaching for his outdoor coat set off in the direction of the village main street on the chance that Julianne might be willing to speak to him on the intercom.

It was not to be so. As he approached the bakery in the shadows on the opposite side of the street the door opened and she came out with a stranger. The two of them were dressed for socialising somewhere in the area and he thought what a fool he was to have been fretting all day because he hadn't been able to apologise about the way he'd treated her the night before and there she was with a spring in her step, smiling up at the fellow.

He stopped and watched as unaware of his presence they walked in the direction of The Mallard, chatting freely as they moved along, and he thought so much for the guilt trip he'd been having. Julianne was like her sister, one man was not enough. Last night must have been just a game she'd been playing. Turning, he went back the way he had come in a night that suddenly felt dark and cheerless in spite of a full moon above.

When Nathan had insisted that she go home because she didn't look well Julianne had been reluctant to do so because it was Aaron's rejection of her and the sleepless night that had followed that were the reasons for her pallid appearance, but she could hardly explain that to the head of the practice because it involved another member of staff, who was also his friend.

So she had done as he had told her to, gone home in the late afternoon, and once George had been given the message to pass on to any callers who might wish to speak to her she had shut herself in the apartment.

When he'd gone to check up on her at closing time he wasn't alone. He had brought someone with him, Mike Mattison, who was married to one of her friends and was the owner of a painting and decorating business in the village.

'I've brought Mike along,' her landlord said, 'as I'm going to have the apartment smartened up for you. It's time it had a fresh lick of paint. He's brought some colour charts for you to look at, and then because I think you need cheering up we're going to take you for a bite in The Mallard, and while we're there you can tell him what you would like.

'If the two of you would like to go on ahead, I'll join you as soon as I've sorted out today's takings. And, Julianne, while you get ready Mike is going to help me decide what to have done at my place.'

Everything that George had said had been uplifting, Julianne thought gratefully as she changed into fresh clothes and repaired her make-up, and when she stood back to admire the effect she was smiling.

Mike and her friend Sallie were happily married and Sallie often said how she wished Julianne could meet

Mr Right and be as happy as they were. Anna, her other friend, said the same thing sometimes and she thought that neither of them knew that she had already met him and there was no joy in it so far.

As they walked the short distance to The Mallard, Mike was telling her how the shop was doing and about the peculiarities of some of the customers, and as she laughed at the stories he had to tell Julianne was thinking that when George joined them she would be with two men that she was comfortable with, that she didn't have to answer to for anything, and the one she longed to be with wanted her far away from him.

They'd been in close proximity all day at the surgery and the only words that had passed between them had been about the patients in their care. Thinking about it, maybe it was just as well. There would be no misunderstandings between them that way.

But when George came bustling into the pub to join them she saw that the clock behind the bar was on seven o'clock and all that she'd just been thinking was forgotten. At this time last night she'd been in Aaron's arms, responding to his kisses, telling herself that it was all coming right at last, and she'd been so wrong. Where was he now? What was he doing? Not fretting about her, that was for sure!

While George was waiting to be served at the bar she asked Mike where Sallie was and he said, 'She's doing a big bake and sent me out of the way. It's my birthday tomorrow and at the last minute we've decided to have a party. We hope you'll be able to come as these sorts of occasions never seem to get off the ground until you arrive.'

'Yes, of course I'll come, winter nights are so dark and long,' she told him, 'but as for my being the life and soul…'

'Well, come anyway,' he told her as George joined them at their table and the talk became about paint and colour schemes. In no time at all the evening had gone and as all three of them had to be up early the next morning Mike said his goodnights and Julianne and George returned to the bakery.

As they separated at the door that led to her apartment above he said, 'By the way, you had a caller as I was putting the shutters up ready for closing. Seemed quite keen to speak to you, but I told him that you didn't want to be disturbed and he went.'

'Who was it?' she asked in combined hope and dread.

'The new doctor. I have to say he seems a decent sort.'

'Yes, he is,' she said slowly, wishing she hadn't told George she didn't want any visitors. She'd just spent the evening with two other men, one of them nearing sixty, and the other her friend's husband, and it had been pleasant enough, but compared to the night before when she'd been taken to the stars for a few exhilarating moments and then plunged back down to earth and reality, tonight had been just one more example of George's concern for her.

'Dr Somerton didn't leave any message, then?'

'No. Were you expecting him to?'

'Not really. We knew each other once long ago and I just wondered, that's all.'

'So that is why he's looking out for you?'

'No, not really,' she informed him, and before he could ask any more questions she wished him good-night and went slowly up the stairs, wishing that George hadn't been so diligent in carrying out her instructions as far as Aaron was concerned.

Aaron finally caught up with her the next morning as they both drove in to the car park of the practice at the same time. His first words were, 'What was wrong yesterday? Why did Nathan send you home, Julianne? Were you ill?'

'No,' she told him. 'He was just being over-cautious. He isn't used to seeing me less than bright-eyed and bushy-tailed.'

'Which I take it was how you always were before I appeared on the scene?'

'Something of the sort, but I'm fine now, and I'm sorry that my elderly protector wouldn't let you get past him yesterday evening.'

'It was all right. I just wanted to apologise for being so pompous and unfeeling when we were at the bistro the night before.'

'I was to blame,' she said, not meeting his gaze. 'We both let our guards down, and I'm sure that you aren't going to let *that* happen again, but, Aaron, please don't leave Swallowbrook because of me. It wouldn't be fair to Nathan and I would feel responsible. I can understand how you feel about my family, but I wish you only happiness. I have no hidden agenda regarding the two of us. I am not like Nadine.'

Cars were pulling up around them as the rest of the staff were arriving. He wanted to tell her he was realising that she was nothing like her selfish sister. He had only to look at her, listen to her, to be achingly aware of the difference, but there wasn't time. Their day was upon them, not only were staff members arriving, patients were appearing too. The Swallowbrook Medical Practice was about to swing into action.

It was like the day before. They had no further chance to talk to each other about themselves, but Julianne was more content knowing that there was a truce between them and every time they came face-to-face Aaron had a smile for her.

In the early evening she dressed to go to Mike's birthday party. She was looking forward to it. She was essentially a party person and loved being with people she knew and liked, and as the folks of Swallowbrook were a friendly lot she was expecting to know most of those who had been invited.

She'd rung Sallie in the lunch-hour to say that she would come early to give a hand with the preparations and by half past six she was on her way to the new detached house that her friends had just moved into.

She was busy in the kitchen, with a large plastic apron covering her dress while she was putting the finishing touches to some of the food that was going to be part of a buffet during the evening, when Sallie came in to say, 'Guess who I invited and didn't think for a moment would come?'

'I've no idea,' Julianne told her as she checked on a dessert that had just come out of the oven.

'Have a guess!'

'Is he royalty?' she asked, amused at her friend's amazement.

'No, of course not, but he puts all the princes and dukes in the shade.'

'Wow! This I must see!' she said laughingly, and opened the kitchen door a fraction.

She let out a gasp. Aaron was there, chatting to a couple of the guests with a glass of wine in his hand and looking exactly how Sallie had described him.

'What is Dr Somerton doing here?' she croaked.

'I had an appointment with him this afternoon,' Sallie explained.

'Why? You're not ill, are you?'

'No. It was just to have my blood pressure checked as it was a bit up for some reason the last time I was there. We got chatting about the village and things in general and Dr Somerton said that he liked the place a lot, but didn't know many of us as yet, so I invited him to the party. I imagine that you will know him already from working at the practice.'

'Er, yes, I do, but not socially,' she said, and wondered what category kissing would come under.

'So you *will* look after him, won't you, after my inviting him out of the blue, even if some of the other guys are queuing up for your attention?' Sallie pleaded.

'I'll do my best,' she said weakly, 'but you know it can happen that being with a person all day in the workplace is enough, without being in their company in the evening too, and I think that the guy in question prefers me in small doses.'

'So he's hard to please,' Sallie said laughingly, and went back to her guests.

More like he has a long memory, Julianne thought, and sallied forth to greet him after removing the apron and taking a quick look to make sure that her dress hadn't suffered in the process.

Aaron was half-turned away from her as she moved towards him and when she touched him on the elbow he turned slowly and there was satisfaction rather than surprise in his smile.

'Hello, there,' he said. 'Has your friend told you that we chatted at the surgery today and I ended up with an invitation to her husband's birthday party, which was very sociable of her, don't you think?'

'Yes, I suppose it was,' she agreed. 'I didn't know about the party myself until Mike mentioned it when George and I were with him in The Mallard last night.

He nodded. 'Yes, I saw you and the birthday boy heading in that direction.'

'How?' she exclaimed. 'When?'

'It was when I was still trying to make my apology for those moments at the bistro, *and* after Helena had told me you'd been sent home because you were unwell.

I was concerned about you being ill all alone in that flat of yours. George said you didn't want visitors the first time I called, and when I saw you going towards The Mallard I had been about to make a second attempt to speak to you.'

'And no doubt when you saw me you must have thought that there couldn't be much wrong with me if I was out for the evening with another man, and that I was following the family trend of loose behaviour.'

The people he'd been chatting to had moved to talk to someone else and they were alone in a corner of the room for a moment.

'And how was I supposed to know who he was?' he asked levelly. 'The reason I am here tonight is because I said to your friend that as yet I know very few of the locals.'

'Yes, well,' she said, brushing what he'd just pointed out to one side, 'I had no intention of going anywhere last night until George came up to the apartment with Mike, who is a painter and decorator, and announced that he had arranged for him to give my apartment a facelift, and the same for his own house next door.

'George insisted that the three of us combine looking at colour charts with some socialising in the pub, and Mike and I went on ahead as George wanted to sort out the takings from the bakery before he joined us.

'And if you are going to ask where Mike's wife was while all this was going on, Sallie was at home here, baking for tonight's party, and had sent him out of the way.'

Julianne knew she sounded defensive, but inside she was aching because he had come to seek her out the night before from concern and contrition and must have wished he hadn't bothered when he'd seen her leaving the apartment smiling and relaxed with another man.

She was right about that. It was exactly how he had felt, but it hadn't stopped him from accepting an invitation from a stranger to a party where local people would be present on the off chance that she might be there, and this time he'd got it right.

She was standing beside him in a pale blue dress that showed off her dark attractiveness perfectly and was wearing high-heeled shoes that gave her another five inches in height so that she came just past his shoulder. As a number of the party guests were observing them curiously he said, 'I've met a few of these folks at the surgery but only briefly, as you can imagine,' and with a glance at George and his lady friend who were at the far end of the room, 'and I already know your protective landlord, but the rest of those here are strangers.'

She smiled up at him. 'So shall I introduce you to those you don't know? I have Sallie's orders that I am to look after you.'

That took the edge off his enjoyment immediately. To be told that the most attractive woman in the room and likely to be in much demand was sticking with him because she'd been told to was humiliating and he said dryly, 'No, don't bother. I will only forget their names and I'm sure that I will be meeting most of your friends at one time or another with their health problems. Time enough to get to know them then.'

He was being churlish and knew it, but how was he to know if the time she was spending with him was a chore or a pleasure after what she'd just said? In any case, he had come to the party for one reason, only to be where she was, not to be shown around like exhibit A.

The colour was rising in her cheeks as she replied, 'Yes, of course. I understand perfectly. I should have realised that you will want to make your own introductions if you feel so inclined. If you will excuse me, I think we are almost ready to eat and Sallie will need my assistance. You will know where to find me if you need me for anything.' *Which I'm quite sure you won't after making it so clear that you don't feel the need to be tied to me for the rest of the evening.*

Aaron was as prickly as a porcupine about anything that placed them together, yet he'd been persistent enough in his efforts to get to see her the night before.

For the rest of the evening she kept her distance and he didn't blame her for doing so. Why on earth had he treated her like that, when all she'd wanted to do was to make him feel welcome amongst strangers?

As the hours went by various people came to chat when they discovered from Sallie or Mike, certainly not Julianne, that he was the new doctor at the practice, filling the gap that Nathan's wife, Libby, had left when their daughter had been born just a short time ago.

But they were not as many in number as the folks who sought out Julianne and encircled her with good-natured banter and lots of laughter. Every man in the place, including himself, found her enchanting, but none of those drawn to her like bees to honey were aware that they had met before, unless she had told them, and he couldn't see her doing that, as she wouldn't come out of it too well.

It was midnight and the party was drawing to a close as most of those present had work to go to the following day, and Aaron waited to see who would see Julianne home.

Not many of the guests had come by car so there would be some going her way, but when he looked around him to see who she was about to walk the short distance with she wasn't there, and following his glance Sallie said, 'Julianne left a few moments ago after refusing several offers of company on the way home.' As he observed her in disbelief she said, 'She often does that, but you might catch her up if you hurry.'

She was talking to his departing back and smiled as she closed the door behind him and went to say goodbye to the last few stragglers.

He caught up with Julianne a hundred yards or so down the road and realised his anxiety was needless. There were enough of the partygoers moving in the same direction for her to be quite safe and as he drew level he wasn't expecting a warm welcome.

'What do you want?' she asked, without turning her head in his direction.

'Nothing special,' he told her, aware that she must think him interfering to be meddling in her affairs to such an extent. 'I just wanted to make sure that you arrived home safely.'

The bakery building was looming up in front of them and pointing to it she said, 'And now you know that I have, so goodnight, Aaron.'

He turned and pointed himself in the direction of the lake and the ever-flowing waterfall, and nodding in sombre acceptance of what she'd said went on his way.

Slowly mounting the wooden staircase once more, Julianne was wishing that they could be in harmony for more than the few seconds that it always turned out to be.

She'd been delighted to see Aaron at the party and would have loved to spend the entire evening with him, but it had seemed that he hadn't shared her feelings and hadn't really wanted to get to know more of the Swallowbrook inhabitants, so why had he come?

Striding homewards briskly, Aaron was telling himself that Julianne must feel that there was something wrong with his thought processes and she wouldn't be far out. By nature he was sensible and reliable, not given to irrational behaviour, but that didn't apply to the present.

He was spending half the time shying away from her and the rest fussing over her wellbeing as if she were some vulnerable teenager when she was nothing of the sort.

Her family circumstances must have left her out on a limb where togetherness was concerned and the result was a woman who had her life organised, could cope with being alone because she'd had to, and so far seemed to be in no hurry to commit herself to any man.

As for himself, he had dreamed of having children to cherish in a childhood that had been going to be so different from his own and had ended up with nothing, neither wife nor child. The party would have been great if he hadn't let his doubts about the wisdom of them being together and moving on to a deeper relationship make him edgy. His wish had been granted. Julianne had been there and what had he done? Passed by the chance to spend some quality time with her.

Concerned that she was walking home alone, he had gone after her at the end of the evening and received the kind of reception he'd deserved. What tomorrow would bring between them at the practice he just didn't know.

As a fitting end to an unsatisfactory evening a vision came to mind of her as a shy teenager in a bridesmaid's dress, with eyes big and questioning but not distraught behind the posy of flowers she'd been carrying and which she had held up to her face to hide behind.

Going morosely up to bed, the last thing that would ever have occurred to him was that it was because *she* was the one who had cared for him and still did, not her money-loving sister.

If he had been expecting awkwardness between them the next morning, he was wrong. After some deep thinking on her part when he had disappeared into the night after her implied rebuke, Julianne had decided that the best way to cope with their closeness at the surgery, *and lack of it in their relationship if it could be called that,* was to stay clear of him in every other situation that occurred where they might be thrown together.

At least he was only on the fringe of her life, she had reasoned. For the last five years she hadn't known where he was. Now she could love him from the side-lines, which was better than nothing. So when he arrived at the practice the following morning she had a smile for him that told him exactly nothing about what she was thinking, but at least there was no coldness in it.

There had been a frost again during the night, not entirely unexpected for the time of year, and as she'd driven to the practice Julianne's composure had wilted at the thought of Christmas in Swallowbrook with the two of them together yet separate at this special time of year.

She had been brought up some miles away, but was always entranced by the magic of the Lakeland village at this time of year with the fells snow-capped and fairy lights and Christmas trees everywhere.

Knowing her friends, there would be lots of parties to look forward to, with the delightful tradition of exchanging presents, and if Aaron was only on the fringe of the festivities by his own choice, at least she would be able to see him and care about him, maybe even get a reluctant kiss from him under the mistletoe.

CHAPTER SIX

THE day progressed like most days in a busy medical centre, with the local population coming and going with their various health problems and the team of doctors and nurses at the ready to treat them.

They were a likeable lot, the staff, with Nathan as head of the practice happily married to Libby and also the loving father of Toby, whom he had been godfather to until the little boy's parents had been lost in a ferry disaster while on holiday abroad.

There had been no close relatives to take the boy who had been rescued, and Nathan's role in Toby's life had changed to that of father instead of godfather because he had adopted him. Now he and Libby had a little one of their own, baby Elsey, and their lives were a blissful foursome.

The other married couple, who were also doctors, had only recently tied the knot and would not be having any children of their own because Ruby Lawrence had a faulty gene. She was a carrier of haemophilia. Ruby and Hugo had decided that kind of risk was not

for them and intended either adopting or fostering at
some time in the future.

Every time Julianne saw the pain in Ruby's eyes
when Libby brought their children into the surgery to
see their father, or there were young ones in the building as patients, she had to admire her for the decision
that she and Hugo had made never to have a child of
their marriage.

Hugo had once told her that his love for his ethereal-
looking wife would support them in the bad times, and
a couple of children somewhere would benefit accord-
ingly one day.

When she thought about Hugo's and Nathan's happy
families Julianne wondered what it would be like to be
part of one herself, to be loved by Aaron and cherished
and protected like Libby and Ruby were. But those sorts
of relationships would be for those who had no iffy track
records as far as he was concerned.

Aaron had been watching Julianne during every free
moment that came his way in the course of the day and
wondering if he was heading for a state of mind and
body that was only happy when he was at the surgery
because it was the one place where Julianne could always be found.

Tomorrow would be when she did her voluntary work
at the hospice in the evening, and when the management
had been in touch to say that they would welcome his
help on the same night as Julianne he had put to one
side his doubts about the wisdom of them being there

together. As they were leaving the surgery at the end of the day he said, 'The hospice has asked me to work the same night as you. I hope you won't find it a problem?'

'It will only be a problem if we make it one,' she told him, her reply giving nothing away.

'Would you like a lift?'

'Er, yes thanks,' she said after a short pause. 'It would be a relief not having to drive.'

Being near him for those few extra hours on that one night of the week would be a mixture of pleasure and pain, but Aaron wasn't going to get to know that as *he* would be putting up with *her* on sufferance.

'Do you have something to eat before you go?' he asked.

She shook her head. 'No. I wait until I have a free moment during the day and pop across to the bakery for a sandwich that I eat on the way. Shall I get one for you?'

'Yes, that would be great if you don't mind' was the reply. 'I'll be waiting in the car park at half past six tomorrow.' And without further discussion he went on his way.

Julianne sighed when he'd gone. Whatever awkwardness their being together at the hospice might cause, their reason for being there was the important thing, giving loving care to those who were weak and ill, whether terminally, or needing a time of quiet and peacefulness in tranquil surroundings.

The following night, after getting the food from the bakery, Julianne was waiting as arranged beside the smart black car that Aaron had bought on his return to the UK.

She had changed out of her surgery uniform and was dressed in sweater, skirt and a warm winter coat, all of which would be taken off and replaced with one of the smart check jackets and the slacks worn by the hospice staff.

Aaron came out seconds after her and as she observed him she thought how calm and controlled he was compared to the jittery half-smile she was bestowing upon him at the thought of being alone in his car with him again.

The memory of the night when they'd gone to The Falls Bistro and she'd ended up in his arms was something she wasn't going to forget in a hurry, although this time they would be travelling through the dark winter night to respond to a different kind of need.

As the powerful car ate up the miles her glance was on his hands on the steering wheel. They were strong and capable-looking with nails neatly trimmed, and with a betrayal of the senses and all logical thought she longed for his touch.

He took his attention off the road for a second and as if he read her mind asked, 'What are you thinking?'

'Nothing,' she told him with false flippancy, 'except maybe that I'm hungry.'

'Well, if you've brought the food we'll stop at the next lay-by,' he said, unaware that it wasn't food that she was hungry for.

She was smiling. 'Not only have I brought sandwiches, I've brought two of George's delicious cream cakes with his compliments and the flask of coffee that he always makes for me when I'm on evening hospice duty.'

'That sounds great,' he said enthusiastically, and within seconds they were pulling up at the side of the road. They ate in silence as if those few brief comments about the food were all they could think of to say, and when they'd finished the cream cakes he took a tissue out of the glove compartment and said laughingly, 'You've got a blob of cream on the end of your nose.'

He leaned towards her and gently wiped it off and with their faces only inches apart it was there again, the chemistry that had propelled her into his arms like a magnet last time.

She drew back, weak with the force of it but still possessing a shred of common sense, and said, 'Thanks for that. The last thing I would want is to arrive at the hospice with cream all over my face.'

'No, of course you wouldn't,' he agreed mildly, as if the kindling of desire had been a one-sided thing, and after draining his coffee cup he set the car in motion once more.

She was acting crazily, Julianne told herself. Only moments ago she had been craving his attention, and when she'd had it she hadn't wanted it. What Nadine did to him had been a long time ago. Surely by now Aaron should be well and truly over it? Although maybe not when he remembered *her* part in it.

Shuddering, she recalled his expression when he'd seen her on his first day at the practice and realised

who she was. Didn't she always get the backlash from
Nadine's selfishness?

Beside her Aaron was also doing some soul search-
ing. So far Julianne appeared to be completely different from her sister, so why couldn't he let the wedding
that never was stay in the past where it belonged and
treat her like any other attractive woman he might meet
instead of being so judgemental?

The hospice was looming up in front of them, bright
lights breaking up the darkness, and with the sight of
it Julianne put all her doubts and uncertainties to one
side. For the rest of the evening it was there her mind
would be focused.

There were those inside the building, recently erected
with funds given to the borough by an unknown wealthy
businessman, who were there to receive the benefit of its
peace and privacy for however long they might need it,
and she always came away with a feeling of tranquillity
that came from having been of help to them.

As they went inside it was immediately obvious that
great care and attention had been paid to the decor and
furnishing of the place, with all woodwork painted in
a matt finish of pale gold and wall and floor areas in
other sunshine colours.

Each patient had their own bedroom with en suite
facilities that looked out onto smooth green lawns, and
as doctor and nurse separated, Aaron to report to who-
ever was in charge and Julianne to go to change into the
uniform that the hospice provided, the evening opened
out before them.

When she reappeared ready for action it was with the satisfaction that she always felt while working there becoming doubled in the knowledge that Aaron was also ready to give his time and knowledge to the hospice.

Life could be so good if he would forgive her for what he saw as past transgressions. But would he ever do that without knowing the truth, that not only had she wanted him out of a marriage with Nadine because it would only have led to great unhappiness for him as her sister had always been a law unto herself with no thought for others, but added to that she, Julianne, had longed for him to look in her direction, but he had barely noticed she was there, having eyes only for the woman he was going to marry.

They met up briefly in the middle of the evening when Aaron came to the section where she was working to examine a patient who was being given morphine to lessen pain and had to sanction an increased dosage of the drug to keep the sick woman comfortable, with Julianne taking careful note of his instructions.

'How's it going?' he asked with a smile that was entirely that of one colleague talking medicine with another, without any depth of feeling other than the importance of the task they had committed themselves to, and she thought that it ought to be enough, but it wasn't.

Since Aaron had come to Swallowbrook life had become a thing of peaks and valleys. Before that she'd been content to exist on the level plane of making the best of what she had, accepting that maybe one day a man might come along who equalled him but never expecting that the real thing would turn up and knock her sideways.

'It's going fine,' she said in reply to his question. 'The regular staff here do all they can to make life pleasant for those in their care and are hugely successful in their efforts.'

She indicated a pale, emaciated-looking woman sitting not far away, who was watching them with bright bird-like eyes that contrasted sharply with her bodily condition and said, 'That is Sabina. She is very sick but won't take her medicine unless we play a CD of Spanish dance music and John the porter and one of the nurses do a tango while she is drinking the offending potion… *in a wine glass*.'

'So she's Spanish?'

'No, but she likes that kind of music.' With a quick change of subject she asked, 'So how has your first evening gone down in this amazing place?'

'Fine,' he said easily. 'The time has gone fast. Another hour and we'll be done.' He looked around him. 'It must be some generous guy who paid for all this.'

'We are told that his father was in the previous building that this one has replaced and although he was well cared for the benefactor felt driven to provide an even better hospice in memory of him and this is it.'

'It's certainly impressive,' he agreed, and went on his way to where he was hoping that the next patient would be willing to take their medication without him having to do a tango for them, like the porter did for Sabina.

* * *

'Will you just be doing the one night each week?' she asked him as they drove back to Swallowbrook later.

'I've been asked if I would be willing to do some Sunday work as well,' he replied. 'Afternoons probably, but I don't want you to feel that I'm crowding you by working the same hours as you at the weekend as well as during the week, and have told them I will think about it.'

'If you can do some good there I wouldn't want you to refuse it on my account,' she told him. 'Feel free to do whatever suits you best.'

'Are you sure?'

Yes, she was sure. He'd mentioned moving on to a fresh practice because of her in one of their less happy moments and with that thought hanging over her the more time she spent with him the better to remember him by.

He didn't linger when he dropped her off outside the bakery and the invitation to come in for a coffee froze on her lips. 'See you in the morning,' he said, and before all his vows to keep a distance from the raven-haired enchantress who belonged more to the past than the present were scattered on the wind, he drove off into the night.

Why had he told Julianne that he might be working Sunday afternoons as well as Thursday evenings? It would have been time enough for her to find out on the day, without having the next forty-eight hours to consider the prospect.

Supposing she'd got the wrong idea, thought he'd

asked for those hours especially? She would be wary of him again, just as they were beginning to melt a little towards each other.

It was true, he *had* been asked to work Sunday afternoons, but only for a few weeks to fill a vacant slot caused by the illness of a member of staff, unlike Julianne's commitment, which was a regular one.

She wasn't filling anybody's empty place, certainly not the one beside him in his bed on the long, lonely, nights that he'd begun to accept as part of life, *his life anyway.*

There was a short practice meeting the following morning when all staff had been asked to be present at eight o'clock, before the surgery opened at half past. It had been arranged by Nathan mainly to officially welcome Aaron and to announce a few items of change that were about to take place in the organisation of the practice.

Although the cancer clinic close by was a separate entity, the two places worked well together and Gabriel was always ready to co-operate with the surgery during meetings about the day-to-day functions of the two important centres of health care in Swallowbrook.

Gabriel was a man of striking appearance and very much in love with his wife if the tenderness in his expression as he observed her was anything to go by.

But her observation of Gabriel and Laura ceased when the man who had *her* emotions see-sawing all the time seated himself a few feet away, after sending a brief smile in her direction. After last night's lukewarm goodbye she wondered what confusion of feel-ings he had in store for her today.

She was soon to find out. After Nathan had made his speech of welcome and expressed his pleasure on ob-serving how well Aaron had settled in amongst them, the man himself got to his feet, thanked Nathan for his kind words and then said, 'You were not all strangers to me when I arrived here. Nathan and I had already met in Africa and Julianne Marshall and I are acquainted from way back through a relative of hers and are get-ting to know each other all over again.'

As the heat of embarrassment stained her cheeks she managed a weak smile and wished herself far away. Why had Aaron said that? Was he wary of someone finding out that they hadn't been strangers on meeting here in Swallowbrook, and did it matter if they did?

She supposed she ought to be grateful that he hadn't embellished the announcement with the circumstances of their previous acquaintance, yet he was hardly going to do that, was he, allow those who knew nothing of it to become aware of his humiliation on a certain day?

It had to be that he'd mentioned it merely as just something to say without consulting her first and there were a few surprised expressions on the faces of those present.

Not on Nathan's, though. His mind was on what he was about to say next and the effect it might have on those involved. 'Some of you may remember that not long ago I mentioned a new arrangement with regard to staffing,' he said, addressing everyone.

'A kind of team arrangement where each of we doctors works with one of the nurses as a pair, except for emergencies,' he explained. 'Such as Helena and myself, Hugo with Gina, who is going to increase her hours to match his, and Julianne with Aaron, who I have discussed it with previously and who, he tells us, are already acquainted.'

With a smile in Ruby's direction he told her, 'We are shortly to employ another nurse, who will work with you, Ruby, until such time that you decide whether or not you want full-time employment, part-time, or to do as Libby has done.

'So, has anyone any comments to make about the new arrangements? The idea behind it is that if the same two people work together as a team all the time it will give our patients even more confidence in our already excellent health care. I intend that it should commence on Monday next.'

There didn't seem to be anyone who wasn't in favour of the new scheme. Everyone was nodding their approval, but with regard to herself Julianne wasn't sure what to think.

She'd let Nathan see that she had her doubts about partnering with Aaron when the subject had come up on an earlier occasion, and if he thought that she and Aaron were big buddies, after him explaining that they were already acquainted, he had another think coming. Their situation was such that she was '*yearning*' and he was '*spurning*'.

But when Aaron came level with her on the stairs

leading up from the basement at the end of the meeting it seemed as if she might be mistaken about that.

'I can't believe that you told everyone we were acquainted from way back,' she said with quiet annoyance. 'Suppose people start asking questions or making enquiries about the past?'

He shrugged. 'If I'm not bothered why should you be? It is done and dusted, Julianne. I've wiped the slate clean. The way ahead is clear.'

Her heart was rejoicing as she swivelled to face him. Was it the moment to tell Aaron that there had never been anything to forgive her for, that she had done no wrong, and none of that mattered now?

The future could be so good, fantastic maybe, if Aaron would let it, and what would be more romantic than love at Christmastime beneath the mistletoe, with a fragrant green spruce tree nearby, decked with bright baubles and dancing coloured lights?

Aaron was watching her face light up because she was happy, but where did they go from here? He'd told Julianne that the barrier that had been there between them was gone, but would he ever want to take that risk again with another member of the same family, even though she was nothing like her sister?

As they separated at the door of his consulting room he said briefly, 'You having said that you didn't mind if I worked Sunday afternoons at the hospice. I've told them that I'm willing to do it, so do you want a lift again?'

She hesitated. 'Er, no, thanks, just the same. When I've finished I eat out somewhere, which saves me cooking, so I need to have my car handy.' And before he could comment she was giving him an apologetic smile and moving towards her own part of the surgery, where she could always be found when needed.

As he watched her go Aaron thought there had been no suggestion that they dine together when they finished at the hospice. Had he imagined that she'd been happy only a few moments ago when he'd said that he was ready to let bygones be bygones?

Needless to say, the thought of them eating together after they'd finished their shift had occurred to her, but she needed time to see if Aaron had really meant what he'd said about a clean slate. It was for him to hand out the invitation to dine if that was the case.

But he'd given her hope and she had waited a long time for that. Having him near on Sunday afternoons was a pleasure that she hadn't anticipated. Having already known that Nathan had partnered the two of them at the surgery, her doubts about that had gone, and she was seeing it as a bonus. Life from now on could get to be wonderful.

Driving to the hospice on Sunday afternoon, Julianne was smiling. As she'd passed The Falls Cottage Aaron had swung out onto the road behind her and now they were driving in convoy, which was almost as good as being in one car.

It was a typical winter afternoon, cold and grey, but the weather wasn't registering. She was happier than she'd been in ages, though she had a long way to go yet to find the kind of love that she'd always dreamed of.

On arriving, they went to find out what their duties were to be for the afternoon and discovered that they would be attending a patient who was the wife of the wealthy patron who had supplied the funds to build the hospice.

'When it was built, he asked that a private ward for himself and his family be included in the structure for their own use if ever the need arose,' the sister-in-charge told them, 'especially with regard to his elderly mother, who has since passed on. Today it is his wife who has been brought in for special care and rest, while he is abroad somewhere on business.

'She tells us that she is unable to get in touch with him, that he is somewhere remote, so he is in for a surprise when he gets home, and not a happy one, I'm afraid. So if you will both pop along there, the staff who are due to be relieved can make their departures after putting you in the picture.'

'Wonder what's wrong with the guy's wife?' Aaron mused as they did as they'd been asked.

'No doubt we will soon find out,' she replied, and thought that the woman in question was very fortunate to have a private ward where she could be cared for to such an extent. For anyone questioning why she'd been brought to the hospice instead of a hospital, there were two possible reasons. Either she was terminally ill or, having available the facility that her husband had requested when the place had been built, had decided to make use of it.

It was luxurious, to say the least, Julianne thought as they entered the outer room, where a senior nurse was waiting to brief them, but they weren't there to admire the fixtures and fittings, their purpose was to care for the sick, whether rich or poor.

When the nurse had gone they went into the room together and as Julianne approached the bed Aaron reached for the patient's notes clipped to the bottom rail.

Dismay hit them simultaneously. Hers as she looked down at the woman lying there with her eyes closed, and his as he read the name at the top of the paperwork he was holding.

He was beside Julianne in an instant and she said, choking on the words, 'It's Nadine, Aaron. Whatever can have happened for her to be brought into here like this, and where is her husband?'

'She suffered a miscarriage followed by surgery and is very low in spirits,' he told her, equally astonished.

'And that's it?' she asked incredulously as shock waves continued to wash over her.

'No, there's more.'

'What is it?'

'According to her notes it says that after the miscarriage there were some gynaecological problems to sort out, which was done in a private hospital with doubts about whether she would be able to conceive again.

'Apparently when she was due to be discharged Nadine refused to go home and insisted that she be brought here to this small private ward that her husband had requested when the hospice had been built.'

'I didn't know about any of that,' Julianne said tearfully. 'Do you remember me telling you that we were never very close? I wonder if our parents know what has happened, and why, for goodness' sake, isn't the man she married here?'

Aaron was bending over the sleeping woman and observing her keenly. 'There's no mention of sedation in her notes,' he commented, 'but she is in a very deep sleep.' He was feeling her pulse and checking her heart rate while Julianne stroked her arm gently and pressed her lips against Nadine's brow.

This was not the sister with the shining gold mop and scarlet mouth she remembered. This Nadine was a defenceless, white-faced woman with lank hair in a hospital bed. She should have been with her in her time of need, whatever that might have been.

When she looked up at Aaron his expression was sombre and there was anger in it. 'If she was my wife I wouldn't want to leave her side for a second,' he said tightly. 'You do well to ask where her husband is.'

Julianne felt herself flinching. 'And now that she *isn't* yours, what do you propose to do?'

'I'll let you know once she's awake.'

Julianne felt utterly miserable. Not only was her estranged sister gravely ill but it seemed that, judging by his reaction, Aaron still harboured feelings for Nadine.

* * *

Nadine awoke when the afternoon had passed its peak and lay observing blearily the nurse and doctor looking down at her.

'Julianne?' she questioned. 'And Aaron! You, of all people! Where have the two of you come from?'

'We both do voluntary work here,' Julianne told her gently, 'and if you are surprised to see us, that is nothing compared to our amazement on finding you here. But where is your husband, Nadine?'

'He's left me,' she said weakly. 'I was pregnant and told him I didn't want the baby, that I've always been scared of childbirth, but Howie thought that was just an excuse, and when I mentioned an abortion he went ballistic and said if I went ahead with it, that would be the end of us. He's obsessed with carrying on the family name.

'I didn't really intend doing anything as final as that, but I was angry that he should issue such an ultimatum and told him I'd booked the abortion, which resulted in him walking out on me and I've heard nothing from him since. He sends me money, but we have no other contact.'

'So he doesn't know that you lost the baby from natural causes rather than an abortion?' Aaron questioned grimly.

Nadine shook her head wearily. 'No. He isn't aware that I was prepared to carry it to full term to please him, but that it didn't work out like that and they say that I might not be able to conceive again due to some problem with my tubes. Enough about me and my sad life. Aaron, tell me about yourself. How do you come to be in the lakes?'

'I'm working as a GP at the same surgery as Julianne and we are doing voluntary work in the hospice on Thursday evenings and Sunday afternoons.'

His glance focused on the slender nurse standing tearfully beside the bed. Julianne could have done without this kind of trauma appearing in her life. There would be none of her family to be there for *her* in moments such as this.

If Nadine's marriage had died, it was most likely of her own making. Yet he couldn't help feeling sorry for the situation Nadine had been left in by the man who had taken her into his world of riches and a doubtful kind of esteem. He must have been a cold fish to leave her in such a situation.

When it was time to make way for the next lot of staff to take over Aaron suggested to Julianne, 'Why don't we have our meal in the restaurant here so that you can go back and spend some more time with Nadine before we have to leave?'

'Yes, all right,' she agreed flatly, still trying to take in the happenings of the last few hours. Incredibly, Nadine had been willing to do something unselfish and give her husband the child he longed for, but it had all gone wrong and for once she wasn't riding on the crest of the wave with everything she could ever wish for, except maybe someone like Aaron, who had been cast aside all that time ago.

The address that Nadine had given the hospice was

of a palatial property just a few miles away that Julianne had known nothing about. The last she'd heard had been that they were living in London. So maybe this was a second home near where her husband's parents had lived…and from the sound of things a very empty one with a husband nowhere to be seen and a wife lying semi-comatose amongst the luxury that she had coveted so badly.

CHAPTER SEVEN

As JULIANNE pecked at her food at a table in the restaurant, Aaron was deciding that whether she wanted him to or not he was going to be there for her in the days ahead.

The Nadine situation had come into her life out of the blue and brought with it worry and tears, and also the surprising revelation that her sister wasn't incapable of considering someone beside herself because she'd been ready to face what to her had been the frightening ordeal of childbirth for the sake of the man she'd married.

All of which would have been a very comforting thought if they hadn't found her in such a weak condition, and until she was stronger and able to sort out her own affairs Julianne was going to have to cope with the stress of it on her own if he didn't do something about it.

From the moment they'd met up again he'd been conscious of how out on a limb Julianne was family-wise, with parents in other parts of the world and Nadine living her own luxurious life with little thought about her younger sister's welfare.

'There is nothing you can do for Nadine tonight,' he

said, 'so why not go home and give yourself time to get over the shock of finding her here? She is being well cared for and I don't mind sitting with her for another couple of hours for company.'

'You would do that after what she did to you?' she exclaimed.

'That is in the past. Life is full of new beginnings. While I'm here I'll see if the hospice has information of any kind that might help us locate her husband as obviously he doesn't know about the miscarriage and the resulting surgery she has needed to have.'

With the feeling that she was becoming the odd one out in a threesome Julianne nodded bleakly. 'In that case I'll go and say goodnight to her and will be off. If there's anything fresh to report, you can bring me up to date in the morning.' And while he was paying for the food they'd had she went quickly to where Nadine was in a half-doze and with a promise that she would be back to see her the following evening planted a gentle kiss on her cheek and left before Aaron appeared.

He still cares for Nadine, Julianne thought bleakly as she drove home along deserted roads. His concern was plain to see, and she felt dreadful for feeling jealous of her sick sister. It was like history repeating itself, Nadine the centre of attention and Julianne on the sidelines.

Aaron had assured her that life was full of new beginnings and she had hoped that meeting up with him was going to be one for both of them, but somehow she didn't think that was what he'd had in mind when he'd said it.

* * *

Bogged down with weariness and worry, Julianne climbed the wooden staircase with leaden feet and once in the apartment slumped down onto the nearest chair and stared into space until the clock on a small table beside her showed the midnight hour, and with no wish to be late at the surgery in the morning she undressed slowly and went to bed.

But a vision of Aaron keeping watch over Nadine in the private ward that she'd chosen in preference to going home to an empty house was keeping her awake. Was it going to be during that quiet time together that her sister would admit to having made a mistake on the day that she'd run out of the church to be with another man?

When they met up at the surgery the next morning Aaron beckoned for her to follow him into his consulting room and once she had closed the door behind her she asked urgently, 'How was Nadine when you left her?' with the memory of how he'd despatched *her* off home with unflattering speed.

'A little better. She had a light supper and after we'd chatted for a while went to sleep again,' he informed her, with his expression softening at the thought of the anxieties that had been thrust upon her. But Julianne's thoughts were on a different track when she saw the look as it brought with it the chilling question—was Aaron on seeing her sister laid so low putting the hurts of the past to one side so he was remembering only the good times?

If Nadine's marriage really had foundered, maybe the way would be open for the two of them to take up where they'd left off. Yet in the cold light of day it seemed crazy to even consider such a thing, even though he had wanted to stay longer. But there was the small matter of the missing husband. Where was he? The sooner they found him, the better.

As if he was tuned in to that particular thought, Aaron said, 'I waited until she was asleep and then went to see if the night staff knew anything about her husband's whereabouts. It seems that they have only recently come to live in the area while keeping on a house in London, but at the moment aren't staying in either residence as she is in here as a private patient and he isn't around. One of the nurses said that Nadine had told her he intends to divorce her but didn't know any details.'

As he observed her he was thinking that persuading Julianne to leave the hospice the night before didn't seem to have done much good. She looked as if she hadn't slept and now for some reason she seemed remote and he wanted to hold her close and tell her that he wasn't going to leave her to cope alone, even though he'd sensed withdrawal in her as if she didn't want him involved in the Nadine saga.

It was almost time for the surgery to open its doors and swing into action, not the moment to bring that subject up, and she was edging towards the door, ready to face the day in the nurse's room, so he let her go with one last comment that had nothing to do with her sister.

With a reassuring smile he said, 'Don't forget that our partnering of each other starts from today.'

She *had* forgotten. The previous night's revelations had wiped every other thought from her mind, but his reminder had put her back on track and when he had to send a patient to her in the middle of the morning with a request that they be prepared for a routine examination to see if there might be a threat of cancer of the colon, his instructions were carried out to the letter but with little conversation between them. After that it was the usual busy Monday that always followed the weekend but with a difference because they were working together as a small team, one to one, and if it hadn't been for Nadine and her problems in the background she would have been content.

Towards the end of the day Aaron sought Julianne out once more, only this time it was to enquire whether she intended to visit Nadine at the hospice.

'Can I give you a lift there?' he suggested. 'It would give you a short time to recharge your batteries before getting to the hospice.'

And you a reason for going to see Nadine again, she thought miserably. 'No, thank you,' she told him abruptly. 'I prefer to go alone.'

'Fair enough, if that is what you want,' he said mildly, 'but, Julianne, I am only trying to help at what must be a very stressful time for you. How long is it since you last saw Nadine?'

'Two years,' she said in the same dismissive tone. 'We saw each other briefly one day when we were both out shopping, but as we had nothing to say to each other it didn't last long. If we hadn't found her at the hospice yesterday, the separation would have continued as the two of us have nothing in common.' *Except you, maybe*, she thought as an iron band of misery clamped around her heart.

'All right, if that is what you want,' he said with the smile gone and his glance questioning her change of attitude. 'In that case I will go alone.'

She almost groaned out loud. It would have been easier to accept Aaron's offer instead of allowing a rift to arise between them, but she knew her sister of old. 'Nadine has to have' she used to call her and if Aaron hadn't been that on their wedding day it didn't say that he wouldn't be it now if her husband carried out his threat.

Driving through the dark night again to the hospice, Julianne was in a sombre mood that turned to contrition when she saw how pleased Nadine was to see her, but when she asked eagerly, 'Is Aaron with you?' and pulled a face when told that he wasn't, Julianne's gloom returned.

'How long do you intend staying here?' Julianne asked as they chatted awkwardly about Nadine's stay in the hospice. 'Won't Howie be concerned if he comes from wherever he has gone and finds you not there?'

'I wish,' Nadine said flatly. 'I think there has been too much damage done to our marriage. When I came in here the other day, life seemed like a black pit that I couldn't climb out of, and then you and Aaron appeared and there was light in the darkness, especially when he told me he had forgiven me for what I did to him.'

'Yes,' she replied. 'It takes a very special man to forgive the sort of humiliation that you heaped on him. You were cheating all the time that the wedding plans were going ahead. I wouldn't want to see you ever again if I was him.'

'All right, I get the message,' Nadine agreed uncomfortably, and in retaliation shot back, 'You had a crush him all that time ago, didn't you? It would seem that it might still there.'

'And how are you feeling today, Nadine?' a voice said suddenly from the doorway, and Julianne's heart missed a beat. *Please don't let him have heard that*, she pleaded silently. So, he had come after all as he'd said he would, even though she'd refused a lift. It looked like she wasn't wrong about the revival of his feelings for her sister.

Perversely she decided to leave Aaron alone with Nadine while she went to the restaurant to make up for missing her evening meal and when she'd finished went to speak to the sister in charge to get a general idea of Nadine's condition.

'There is basically nothing wrong with your sister now except exhaustion,' she was told, 'brought on by the mental stress of the miscarriage and the surgery that was needed afterwards, and of course her husband not being around to support her through it all. She could go home any time but isn't planning to do so because she doesn't want to be alone. If you could accommodate her, it might be a solution to her problems but obviously that is a matter for the two of you to decide.'

At the end of the discussion Julianne went back to the small private ward at a slow pace and tried to visualise Nadine slumming it in the small apartment that was so dear to her heart *and so near The Falls Cottage where Aaron could be found.*

Aaron glanced at her questioningly when she reappeared and commented, 'I was about to come in search of you, Julianne. Are you all right?'

'Yes, I'm fine. I've been having a chat with the sister,' she told him breezily, her expression showing no sign of the sacrifice she was contemplating and was about to bring into the conversation immediately as there was no way she could sleep on the suggestion without having tested Nadine's *and Aaron's* reactions to it.

He was observing her doubtfully as she told them, but not so Nadine. She could almost hear the wheels turning in her mind as she considered the suggestion, and Julianne said, 'The apartment is of average size but there is only one bed, so you can have it. I would use a blow-up mattress that I have for when any of my friends stay the night.'

She knew she was crazy to make it so easy for Nadine to infiltrate what had been her happy existence before all this. Bringing her into Aaron's radius and letting her sister use her precious apartment to convalesce would be like handing them on a plate the opportunity to rekindle the romance that Nadine had destroyed that day in the church.

'I have a better idea,' he said immediately, when she'd finished speaking. 'Why don't you go to stay with Nadine? I'm sure she will have much more room in her house than you have in the apartment, as long as it isn't too far for you to get to the surgery.' He turned to her sister. 'Where is it, Nadine? And would you be able to face going back there if Julianne went with you?'

'It's a large manor house in its own grounds called Fellside, and is situated between here and Swallowbrook,' she said listlessly, 'and, yes, I could cope with going back there if I had company.' To Julianne she said, 'It wouldn't be more than a couple of miles away from the surgery for you.'

'I suppose I could stay with you until your husband comes back,' Julianne said with the feeling that she was being uprooted and demoralised with a speed that was leaving her breathless. Why hadn't Aaron wanted Nadine to be as near him as she could possibly get without actually moving in? Maybe he thought that visiting her at Fellside would be more discreet than in the village.

And did he care that he was reorganising *her* life, whether she wanted it or not, that in a matter of hours she had moved from unwanted member of a trio to chaperone and carer in a place where she would be isolated far away from her apartment, her friends and the kindly George?

Aaron was just too bossy for words! Yet she had to hand it to him, his suggestion would make caring for

Nadine much easier in her own home and they would have to take it from there, day by day, night by night. But what if her husband came back? She could be for ever on the sidelines if he didn't.

They left Nadine looking more cheerful than before and went to find their cars for the return journey to Swallowbrook, but before they set off Aaron said, 'I hope you didn't mind my suggesting that you stayed at Nadine's place instead of her at yours. I know how you love your apartment but it just wouldn't be big enough for the two of you for any length of time.'

'Maybe you're right,' she said stiffly, 'but the next time you decide to reorganise my life, maybe you will give me some warning.'

'I'm sorry,' he said apologetically. 'It was just that I felt she would be better in her own surroundings and that it would be less stressful for you that way.'

She got into her car, swinging her legs over the side and settling herself in the driver's seat, and as the engine chugged into life she looked up at him standing beside her and said without replying to his last comment, 'Goodnight, Aaron.' And before she broke down and started weeping at the thought of being banished so quickly from all the things she loved best, she was off. The tail lights of her car glowed in the darkness.

Of course she was willing to look after Nadine until she was fully recovered, but would have preferred to have more time to adjust to the unexpected development in her life without Aaron throwing her in at the deep end before she'd faced up to what it meant.

She was a nurse, for heaven's sake, pledged and trained to care for the sick and suffering, and at the present time that described Nadine, so it went without saying that she would be there for her. But she was nervous at the thought of moving into someone else's house when its owner wasn't there, and wary of being the everlasting onlooker again if Aaron was going to be on the scene all the time.

On a lonely stretch of road with not a sign of civilisation anywhere, the car bumped to a jerky halt and refused to budge any further.

This is the last straw, she thought, *the last, joyless moment of a miserable evening.* Why couldn't it have happened near a garage or when Aaron was with her? No, that would have been too easy. She was alone in pitch darkness without a clue about what was wrong with the car that always served her so well.

She prayed that Aaron would be somewhere behind her on his journey home. Yet supposing he'd taken another route, or gone for a coffee or something similar before setting off?

The bare branches of trees showed up gauntly against the light of a fitful moon that had appeared from behind cloud as she searched for her breakdown details in the glove compartment, and an owl hooted somewhere nearby.

When she found the card with the telephone numbers that she needed she couldn't see it as the electrics of the car were not working and the moon had disappeared again. Laying her head against the steering wheel in utter weariness, she gave in and let the tears flow that she'd been holding back all night.

Aaron had been intending to follow Julianne home as closely as he could get to make sure that she arrived safely, but when he went to get his car, which was in a different parking area from where hers had been, he found that someone had blocked him in and it took precious minutes to find the other driver and get them to move their vehicle.

Then he was off, driving along the same route that Julianne would have taken, expecting that she would be too far ahead by now to catch up, until he saw the outline of the car in complete darkness in the light from his headlamps and pulled up immediately with his heart pounding anxiously.

She was inside, slumped over the wheel, and when he said her name softly she raised her head slowly, burst into tears for a second time and croaked, 'I thought you would never come.'

'I was delayed by the thoughtlessness of others,' he told her in the same gentle tone, 'and the first thing I intend to do is transfer you to my car where there is light and heat, and then I'll have a look at yours.'

When she was standing beside him at the roadside, tearstained and woebegone, she said weakly, with her voice thickening, 'That was so scary, Aaron. I had my breakdown details in the car to call them out to me, but couldn't tell what they were because it was so dark.'

'Come here,' he said, holding out his arms, and she

went into them, knowing there was no other place on earth where she would rather be. As she nestled against his chest with the dark gloss of her hair resting beneath his chin, Aaron brushed his lips against it and held her closer in the magic of the moment.

But he had promised her light and heat and they were not to be found here in the chilly night air, he thought, and releasing her reluctantly he pointed to his car. 'I've got a flask of coffee in there that I brought with me in case I felt thirsty as, like you, I didn't have time to eat or drink before I left the surgery, so you can have a warm drink while I look at your car, and by the way mine has got heated seats so what could be better?'

'I was driving along as normal when it just cut out and stopped,' she said, with the thought that the warmth of his arms was preferable any day to a heated car seat and a flask of coffee. But those kind of moments with Aaron belonged only to times of stress and were brief to say the least, as tonight had shown in spite of her having agreed to move in with Nadine and commute each day from Fellside to the surgery in Swallowbrook.

It was an arrangement that had made her feel that he was willing to manipulate her own movements for the good of her sister, that she was just there to be used and confused.

Yet she could forget all of that in the joy of him having found her and being there to offer comfort in her distress. She was sipping the coffee seated on the warm car seat that he'd promised when he came over to say, 'I've phoned your breakdown people and they are on their way, but they did say that it might take them an hour or so to get here.

'It does seem as if it might be something serious that's wrong with the car but they should be able to enlighten us with regard to that. I'm used to tinkering about with my own cars but this is something out of my league. If I had to make a guess I would think it's to do with the fanbelt.'

Her distress was returning. 'I can't be without it if I'm going to be driving there and back each day from this place where Nadine lives.'

'I will chauffeur you around if need be,' he said reassuringly, 'and in the meantime I suggest that we make ourselves as comfortable as possible until help arrives.' And with a thoughtfulness that almost brought the tears back, 'I'm aware that you have been on your feet all day at the practice and spent the evening visiting your sister. You must be exhausted, so why don't we settle ourselves on the back seat and I'll cover you with the tartan rug that I keep on it for emergencies?'

As they did as he'd suggested Julianne was telling herself that she was asking for trouble. They were too near, too close for sensible behaviour. She wanted him so badly and when he reached out for her suddenly, as if she had in some way communicated her longing to him, he responded with kisses that made her heart beat faster and her body become an offering born of her love for him.

Yet unbelievably he was letting her go, telling her

hoarsely, 'I can't believe I did that. I'm sorry, Julianne. Petting in the back seat of a car is not what I'd intended.'

The heat of her arousal was turning to chill as she said in a low voice, 'I see. And what exactly was it that you *had* intended? Using me to get to her?'

Any further hurt from their brief passion in the back of the car when his moment of desire had changed to regret was prevented by the earlier than expected arrival of the breakdown crew and they at least had nothing to say that could make her feel any more dejected.

Their verdict was that the straps that held the fan belt in position had snapped. She was told that it wasn't a big job that was needed, but it would have to be done at a garage and they would tow the car to the nearest one for what should not be an expensive repair.

They waited until the car and breakdown vehicle had disappeared and then began the rest of their homeward journey, with Aaron commenting how fortunate it was that the fault that had brought her to a standstill hadn't been any worse.

She didn't reply, just nodded, and he knew that he'd rejected something that was new and precious because of that other rejection long ago, and why make Julianne suffer for that? Why be so reluctant to admit to himself that he loved her? Everything about her was entrancing. The last thing he would ever want was that he should be the one who dimmed her light. Nathan and the rest of them at the practice wouldn't want their 'bright morning star' to become just a glimmer because of him.

He knew that Julianne thought he had been fussing

over Nadine since they'd met up again, as if he was some sort of pathetic no-hoper who was willing to risk being cast aside again. As if!

She couldn't be more wrong. His concern was for her. Of course he was sorry that Nadine's life was in such chaos. She'd lost the child she had been expecting and not by her own doing. Nature had had a hand in it, and her husband, wherever he might be, had no knowledge of what had been happening.

Julianne, innocent of all of that, had walked into the mess that her sister had made of her life, and she'd got it wrong if she thought that he would put Nadine first in his concerns.

When they arrived at the bakery it was gone midnight and not another word had been said by either of them until she broke the silence when he pulled up outside by saying tonelessly, 'Thank you for being there for me out in the dark, Aaron.'

Before he could reply she was out of the car, her key was in the lock, the door was swinging inwards, and she was gone into the haven that she was going to have to leave for she didn't know how long.

The next morning George waylaid Julianne as she was leaving for the practice and asked, 'What was going on last night? You went out in your car and came back in Dr Somerton's in the early hours?'

'Mine broke down and had to be towed away,' she told him jadedly, and managed a wintry smile when he commented that the doctor seemed like a good person

to have around in an emergency, and that it was surprising that someone like him wasn't settled with a nice
wife and a couple of young 'uns.

All of that did nothing to lighten a grey November morning that started with the news that Aaron and
Hugo had diverted to Swallowbrook Community Centre to look over a group of young people from a school
in another county who had been lost on the fells overnight with their teacher and were now being checked
for hypothermia and stress while warm blankets and
hot drinks were being provided by local people.

'I told them that you would join them as soon as you
appeared,' Nathan told her. 'So far they haven't found
any youngster needing hospital treatment as they were
all sensibly clothed and there was no frost last night,
but some of the girls are a bit weepy as it can be scary
up there in the dark, so they'll be happy to have the
company of a nurse alongside the doctors, and in the
meantime Ruby and I will hold the fort here until the
lot of them have been given the all clear.'

She had to walk along the lakeside to get to the community centre just a short distance away and as always
was captivated by the beauty of its calm waters nestling
at the foot of the fells.

There were residences on the far side where people
lived in smart detached houses with their own landing
stages and mooring posts, and in the middle on a small
island was the house that belonged to Libby and Nathan,
which could be seen from all angles.

They'd had their wedding reception there and the

two of them and their children now spent most of their weekends on the island.

It was all a far cry from a flat above the bakery but she didn't envy anyone their possessions. She'd been totally happy with her life in Swallowbrook until Aaron had appeared and filled her heart with all the longings of before that were so much deeper now that she'd met him face-to-face again after the long and painful absence that she'd thought had taken him out of her life for ever.

A small motor launch was passing. In it were two of the guys from the group that she socialised with and one of them shouted across, 'Where've you been, Juli-anne? We've missed you at the pub.'

'Family matters!' she called back across the water.

'Not pregnant, are you?' the other one teased.

'No. Adult family matters.'

'Difficult to know which is worse,' he parried, and then they were gone, cutting through the water in the direction of the moorings at the far end of the lake without a care in the world, and she thought that was how she used to be, a pleasure-loving free spirit, until the past had caught up with her and a heart condition known as 'love' had taken over her life.

CHAPTER EIGHT

WHEN Julianne arrived at the community centre to a scene of organised chaos where young people, looking tired and bedraggled, were standing in groups, eating and drinking what the village folk were providing for them, she found Aaron and Hugo amongst them, making sure that none of them were any worse for their ordeal.

As she joined the two doctors Aaron looked up from examining the arm of one of the young boys where a nasty cut was to be seen, and as their eyes met she saw the unspoken questions that the night before had left.

Where do we stand now, his dark gaze was asking, and *am I still the tactless oaf who upset you*? But when he spoke it was about the boy, who was grimacing with the pain from the injury to his arm.

'Nurse Marshall, this young man is our first real casualty so far,' he told her. 'He needs to have stitches in this nasty gash on his arm, so will have to be taken to A and E at the hospital. Fortunately it is only a matter of minutes from here, so would you mind asking the teacher to come over while we sort something out?'

'The coach driver has been here all night, waiting to take them back to where they've come from, so maybe he could stop off at the hospital and the person in charge can take our young casualty to have his arm seen to while the coach waits outside with the rest of them.'

'I imagine they'll give him a tetanus jab while he's there. It's quite a deep cut as he fell on rocks in the dark up on the fells and is quite grimy. The vicar's wife wanted to bathe it but I would rather it was attended to by the hospital right from the start.'

So far Julianne hadn't spoken, but now she broke her silence to say, 'I take it that the teacher is the guy looking so harassed?'

'You take it right,' he said, still with his questions about the night before unanswered, and she thought that was how it was going to stay.

She didn't want to hold an inquest on the humiliation that had been heaped upon *her* this time. Aaron of all people knew what it felt like to be treated as surplus to requirements.

Loving him was just too complicated, she'd decided in the last moments before a restless sort of sleep had closed in on her during the night. She would be back with her friends on the merry-go-round the first chance she got, but that thought had passed as quickly as it had come. She wasn't going to be around socially for some time if she was caring for Nadine.

Her sister needed her and poles apart though they might be she knew that Aaron's suggestion that she stay with her until she was strong enough to take up the reins of her life again was the sensible and most charitable thing to do, because if she tried to get in touch with their parents it didn't mean that they would come rushing to be with their eldest daughter in her time of need.

But that jumble of thoughts had been there during the night and now in the clear light of day she was pushing them to the back of her mind for a short time as the hospice had rung to say that her sister was not being discharged until the following weekend at her own request, so there would be a breathing space before she had to leave the apartment for she didn't know how long.

The coach party had left, aiming first for the hospital before starting their homeward journey, and the doctors and nurse were free to return to their normal duties at the practice.

Hugo had driven Aaron and himself to the community centre and as he was aiming to visit a patient on the return journey it left Julianne and Aaron to walk back the way she had come.

A chill wind was rippling the still waters of the lake now and she thought how in keeping with her mood it was, but Aaron had another card to play to make up for getting it all wrong. Whether it would turn out to be the ace of hearts he wasn't sure, so the best thing was to say his piece and see what sort of a reply he got.

'The letting agent who acts for the people who own The Falls Cottage has been in touch to say that they want to sell it, that it will be going on the market soon, and are asking if I would be interested in buying it before it is advertised.'

'Really?' she exclaimed with muted interest. 'And are you?'

'What? Interested? I suppose I could be. It's a very attractive property. You haven't seen the inside, have you?'

'No,' she replied, 'but if it is anything like the outside I'm sure it must be delightful.'

'Yes, it is. We'll be passing it in a few moments. Would you like to have a quick look around just to satisfy your curiosity? I'm sure they can spare us for a few moments longer at the surgery.'

'Er, yes, I suppose so,' she said half-heartedly, with the last time they'd been in close contact too clear for comfort.

When they arrived Julianne paused to watch the waterfall for a moment as it came down the hillside on its headlong journey into the lake, and as she looked around her she thought that the cottage was in a heavenly place. Turning to Aaron who was taking note of her expression, she said, 'How did you find this place?' You signed up to rent it while you were still abroad, didn't you?'

'I asked Laura if she would find me somewhere to live when I arrived in Swallowbrook and she sent brochures from local estate agents. Once I'd seen the one for this place I didn't look any further, but you are here to see what it's like inside.' He opened the door and ushered her in out of cold.

'It is a mistake to describe this beautiful house as a cottage,' she told him after the first few moments of viewing what so far had been his temporary home, but she was turning to go. 'I don't want to see any more, Aaron, or I might fall out of love with my apartment. Yet it is said that home is where the heart is and that is certainly where mine is.

'But don't let me discourage you from buying this lovely place if you intend staying in Swallowbrook. You must remember, though, that you were dismayed to find me already living here when you arrived, and added to that during the last few days Nadine has surfaced not too far away and nothing has changed much where she is concerned. In spite of losing her baby and the disappearance of her husband, she is still "Nadine has to have".' *And I can't bear the thought that 'having' you once again might be on her agenda.*

'It only needs my parents to turn up,' she went on to say, 'and the whole of my dysfunctional family will be blundering into your life, whether you like it or not. It is my mother that Nadine gets her desire for the luxuries of life from, and my father sails the seas in a beautiful yacht all the time as a way of avoiding family responsibilities. So think carefully before you buy this beautiful home. I would hate to have to watch it grow sour on you.'

When she'd stepped over the threshold of The Falls Cottage Aaron had been smiling because he'd been expecting Julianne to be as impressed with the house by the waterfall as he was, and if that had been the case he would have invited her to somewhere much more special than the back seat of his car, where he would have asked her to marry him, but what she'd just said had left his hopes of her feeling the same as he did—in fragments.

He didn't care a damn what her family were like, had already had the stuffing knocked out of him by one of them five years ago, and her description of the older generation fitted in more with the word 'parents' than Mum and Dad.

But they and Nadine were not the ones he wanted to love and cherish for the rest of his life. Tolerate maybe, he would do that for Julianne's sake, but she was going to need some convincing that it was the right thing to do if he asked her to marry him. From what she'd just said, she was light years away from thinking along those lines.

As they walked the rest of the way in another of the silences that seemed to come so often upon them, he thought wryly that he would live anywhere that she wanted if only she loved him, even in the apartment above the bakery if that was what she wished. At least up there they wouldn't have to go far for fresh bread, and maybe the genial George would walk the bride down the aisle if her yachtsman father didn't make it.

But it seemed as if there might be a long way to go before any of that happened, if it ever did, and when the surgery came into sight it was a reminder that there were those inside whose problems were of the present rather than the future.

As Julianne went to join the other two nurses she couldn't believe that she had spoiled Aaron's pleasure in showing her around somewhere that he had seemed keen to make his permanent home. She'd used the short-comings of her family as a deterrent when in truth she was still smarting at the way he'd put her from him in his car the night before as if she was bad news, or maybe he'd sensed a honey trap of some sort.

They'd had to pass The Mallard on the way back to the practice and she'd glanced across at it edgily. Life had been easy and uncomplicated not so long ago, no unrequited love to contend with or passion that came out of nowhere and turned her into a heap of yearning.

Yet it had also sometimes been boring, with the same friends in the same places. So why had she behaved like someone with no interest whatsoever in being part of Aaron's life, when in truth she would be ready to live anywhere with him if he would only ask her?

But was it her that he would want to live with him in the beautiful lakeside property? She'd seen his concern when they'd discovered that Nadine was their patient the other night, and he hadn't hesitated in suggesting that she, Julianne, should move in with her into what would undoubtedly be a pretentious property in a se-lect position, making her own little haven seem like a hen cote. If Howie didn't show up soon, her sister might reveal just how much her affections were on shifting sands with Aaron around all the time.

Unaware that her mind was on other things when she appeared in the nurses' room, Helena said, 'Don't forget the Snow Queen procession on Saturday, Juli-anne. Sophie Armitage, Laura and Gabriel's nine-year-old daughter, is to be the queen and needless to say our practice manager is highly delighted and so is the Angel Gabriel, as her father is known to some of his grateful cancer patients.

'Sophie will be touring the village with her attendants dressed as snowflakes on a sleigh pulled by two of the horses from the riding school, and will be crowned in the village hall by Libby Gallagher, with her own little snowflake, baby Elsey, close by.

'After the crowning ceremony there will be hot soup and bacon rolls in the village hall, making the whole thing a very fitting occasion for this time of year. But we do need some snow to make the day complete and although the weathermen are hinting at it, nothing definite has been promised.

'Dr Somerton is going to be there, he's keen to be involved in the life of Swallowbrook apart from what he does here at the practice, so you will have company.'

I wouldn't be too sure about that, Julianne thought. *After what I said earlier. I would expect Aaron to run a mile in the opposite direction if he sees me coming on that day.*

He appeared at that moment with a request for the records of a patient that appeared to be missing from the pile in front of him on his desk, and was told that Gina, one of the two nurses left to hold the fort while Julianne had been at the community centre, had seen the patient earlier for an injection and Aaron was questioning if that had anything to do with the misplaced records.

He glanced briefly in Julianne's direction and she

longed for there to be harmony between the two of them in spite of her doom-and-gloom attitude of earlier.

She'd wanted any time she spent with Aaron to be happy and carefree. Having him so near after such a long absence from her life would be magical if only there were no side issues such as Nadine's health and happiness and her sister's uncertain future, and there was also the state of her own life to consider, which could hardly be described as contentment.

They were still going to see Nadine each evening, Aaron and herself in their separate cars, as the repair to hers had been as the breakdown company had foretold, less serious than it had at first appeared.

There was still no sign of the man her sister had rejected Aaron for and the days were drawing nearer to her return to the empty house that she had been dreading so much until she, Julianne, had fallen in with his suggestion and was going to be there with her.

But before the Sunday of Nadine's discharge from the hospice there was the Snow Queen celebration on the Saturday and though the cold was strengthening there was still no sign of the soft white flakes falling from the sky that would make the day complete.

On the Friday night when Julianne went to see Nadine she asked her if she would like to go to the crowning the following day. 'It is in the afternoon and I could come for you and take you to Swallowbrook where it will be taking place,' she coaxed, observing that her sister was already shaking her head at the idea, and she wondered if it was because Aaron wasn't there to offer his persuasion.

It was the first time he'd missed an evening visit, the reason being that he was helping the organisers of the yearly event to erect a raised platform in the village hall for the Snow Queen's throne, and his absence had been noted with obvious disappointment by the woman who had once passed him by for what she'd seen as a bigger fish and was coming to realise that what she'd caught in her net might turn out to be just a small one.

'Just be sure to come for me on Sunday,' Nadine said in the form of a refusal. 'The trivia of village life does not appeal to me.'

'I'm not likely to forget Sunday, am I?' Julianne commented with a vision of the apartment that would be denied her presence in days and weeks to come.

Reading her mind, Nadine was observing her scornfully. 'You'll soon forget that box of a place where you live when you see Fellside,' she announced, and Julianne thought grimly that the only thing that would cause her to go into raptures would be the arrival of the missing husband to take up his responsibilities towards his wife.

When Julianne awoke on Saturday morning thoughts such as those were far from her mind. A fine white carpet lay over the village. During the night the elements had been kind to the youthful Snow Queen and her attendants and everyone was smiling at the gift from above.

As if that wasn't enough to bring rejoicing, Aaron

phoned early to say that if she was going to be on her own at the event he would be looking out for her where the procession was due to commence on the lakeside after the queen and the rest of the young girls had finished sailing round the lake on one of the big launches that were always to be seen on its waters.

Once they had left the launch the local brass band would take over and lead the way to the village hall for the crowning, and as Julianne's gaze searched the crowd for him amongst those waiting to see them set off he appeared beside her and made her day complete.

He was observing her laughingly and commented, 'No need to ask if you are well covered against the cold. I love the woolly hat and mittens...' he touched her face gently '...and the rosy cheeks.'

It felt as if the moment was wrapping itself around her like soft cashmere until he asked casually, 'So how was the patient when you saw her last night?' And suddenly the fabric felt rough and repellent.

Drawing away from his touch, she said, 'I offered to bring Nadine here today but she refused, didn't want to be involved in "village trivia".'

'That is her loss, then,' he said casually, but she saw that a frown was creasing his brow and thought surely it wasn't because Nadine had refused her offer, knowing her it wasn't entirely unexpected.

'And what about tomorrow?' he asked, with more urgency.

'No problem there. She's looking forward to going

home now that she won't be alone,' she told him, and saw that he was smiling.

'That's good.'

'Yes, I suppose it is. I can't let her be in what sounds like a big place on her own, and mine is too small, so...'

'Exactly,' he agreed and as the band struck up and the procession began to move off, 'and tomorrow is another day. Today is ours, Julianne, are we agreed on that?'

'I suppose so,' she told him, 'but before it gets under way, can I say something?'

'Yes, as long as it doesn't spoil it for us.'

'You have already done that.'

He was swivelling to face her. 'How? What have I done to make you say that?'

'You turned us into a threesome by asking about Nadine.'

'That was the doctor in me surfacing,' he protested incredulously. 'Surely you understood that? I can't believe it if you didn't.'

'I didn't, I'm afraid,' she said remorsefully, 'and now I'm the one who has spoiled the day.'

'Why don't we call it quits,' he said mildly, 'pick up the pieces and start again? I know you must feel that Nadine is a blight on your life in spite of your concerns about her welfare. So if I might be allowed to repeat myself, today is ours. Agreed? And if we don't get a move on, we will miss the crowning.' Taking her hand in his, he broke into a sprint to catch up the tail end of the band as it disappeared round the next corner.

* * *

In spite of the shaky start, incredibly it *was* their day, and Julianne thought if it was the only quality time she ever spent with Aaron it would be something to treasure always. His amazement on discovering that she'd thought he still had feelings for Nadine had bordered on the ludicrous, as if any other serious attachments with her family would be strictly taboo, and she'd contributed to that the other day by giving him the low-down on their faults and failings.

But this day, this special, fantastic day that they had claimed as their own, would be engraved on her heart for ever. They had walked hand in hand on the soft white carpet beneath their feet, and been touched by the childlike dignity of the young snow queen and her attendants as they had taken their places on the makeshift stage.

For a moment Julianne had let herself dream what a child of theirs would have been like if she hadn't been tainted by the deeds of others. She had never forgotten Aaron's anger that day in the church when Nadine's departure had resulted in she herself looking relieved in the midst of his humiliation.

She'd expected him to have mentioned it when they'd first met up again, but either he had forgotten it or had written it off as just another indiscretion of the family he'd been intending marrying into.

Now they were in a queue in the village hall where the hot food was being served, and the magic was beginning to fade. It was late in the afternoon and soon it would be dark. The crowning of the Snow Queen would be over and so would their time together in wonderful harmony as there was no plan for them to spend what was left of the day with each other.

When they arrived at the food counter George was beaming at them from behind it. Much of the food had been prepared in the bakery and so he was in charge and approved of what he was seeing as they approached.

But Julianne felt like telling her kindly landlord that he was on the wrong track and Aaron's mind was focusing on what he intended saying to her next, so for George the moment was losing its promise.

'How about we go for a meal this evening as a fitting end to the day?' Aaron suggested when they'd been served. 'We've both time to go home and change and I'll pick you up at seven o'clock, say.'

Her sparkle was back. 'That would be perfect. Heaven knows when I will be free for anything like that once I'm installed at Nadine's house.'

'Don't forget that I've offered to do the chauffeuring there and back for you,' he reminded her. 'I've developed a guilt complex ever since suggesting that you move in with her.'

She was smiling. 'It is the right thing for me to do, Aaron, so don't feel guilty. Blood is thicker than water and we *are* family, so don't give it another thought.' *But just as families can bring joy to our lives, so sometimes they can blight them. I don't expect you to ever want me as much as I want you.*

Her smile was steady, giving no hint of the hurt behind it, and it was only when they separated to prepare for the evening ahead that it disappeared.

She had showered and was now standing in front of the open wardrobe in her bedroom. What to wear was the question for an evening to be spent with her dream man.

Something smart and plain, or flowery and flattering, maybe? Not too over the top for a local restaurant but attractive enough for Aaron to think she looked beautiful in it.

But as she stretched up to lift down a dress of apricot silk that always enhanced her dark attractiveness Julianne became still, with the dress on its hanger dangling loosely from her hand.

Did she want to endure the pain of dining with Aaron in what would be a charade on her part? she thought. A mixture of pleasure and the grim reality that *her* role in his life would always be that of the sister of his runaway bride and as such not for him?

Hanging the dress back in the wardrobe, the decision was made.

Before she weakened and changed her mind she picked up the phone and when he answered told him, 'I hope you will excuse me, Aaron, I'm going to give the meal a miss and have an early night to get ready for tomorrow's upheaval.'

'Fine, if that is what you want to do,' he said evenly, his glance on the jeweller's box that held the solitaire diamond ring that he'd been hoping to put on her finger before the evening was over as a fitting end to a very special day and the beginning of a life with the woman he hadn't been able to stop himself from falling in love with.

Was it going to be that Julianne had her sister's talent for picking him up and putting him down when it suited her? She'd been totally happy all the time they'd been together at the Snow Queen's crowning and afterwards, but it would seem that once he was out of sight she wanted him to stay there.

However, he did have one last comment to make. 'I promised that I would be there to help when Nadine leaves the hospice and have no intention of changing my mind, so don't think of cancelling that arrangement too.'

'No, of course not,' she agreed stiltedly. 'I need to find out what time she intends to leave there and will let you know.'

'No need to do that. I'll give her a ring in the morning to check if she wants me to go on ahead and make sure that the heating has been left on. Moving into a cold house won't do her any good in her present condition, and once again, Julianne, it is the doctor in me surfacing, nothing else, and now don't let me keep you from your early night.'

Before she could tell him with dwindling determination that all she would ever want was to be with him, he rang off and a miserable silence descended upon the apartment.

It lasted until two o'clock in the morning when the phone on the bedside table rang. When she raised herself upright off the pillows and picked up the receiver

George's voice came over the line and he was gasping for breath.

'George! What's wrong?' she cried.

'I've got a heavy pain in the middle of my chest,' he croaked, 'and my heart is banging all over the place. Can you come and see if I need to ring for an ambulance?'

'From the way you sound, I would say yes, you do,' she told him. 'I'll be with you in a moment. I'll come down the back stairs. Is the door open?'

'Yes, and I phoned Dr Somerton for *his* advice too and he's on his way.'

She was checking George's heartbeat, which was dangerously uneven as was his pulse, when Aaron came striding into the bedroom.

'I told George not to disturb you,' he said in a low voice as he stopped beside her, 'but obviously he did.'

'Of course he did!' she exclaimed, moving over so that he could do his own assessment of the distressed baker. 'He is the kindest of men and my friend. In the time I've known George I've seen more of him than I ever have of my father.'

Aaron was only half listening. He knew a heart attack when he saw one and George had all the signs. 'Julianne, phone for an ambulance and tell them not to waste any time,' he said tersely.

George's breathing was still ragged and painful and they noted that his feet and ankles were swelling. 'Are they usually like that?' Aaron asked, and she shook her head.

'Not that I've noticed…and I'm going with him when the ambulance comes.'

He didn't argue. Instead he said, 'I'll come too for moral support, so go and get dressed as quickly as you can before it gets here. I'll look after George.' The baker cried out from the pain in his chest. 'Let's hope they won't be long! He needs to be assessed for a myocardial infarction and treated fast. The sooner he's on treatment the better his chances of recovery.'

She dashed up to the apartment and threw on a sweater and jeans, grabbed a warm jacket out of the wardrobe and was back with them when the sirens of the ambulance could be heard as it came along the road outside the bakery.

From then on it was action stations as the paramedics took over, with Julianne hovering anxiously beside George and Aaron praying there wasn't going to be heartbreak ahead for her if her landlord didn't survive the attack.

They were giving him oxygen to help his breathing and as she watched over him Aaron heard her whisper, 'Why are those I love always lost to me?'

What was that supposed to mean? he wondered, longing to hold her close and comfort her. Julianne was afraid that she might lose George, but he would be on the cardiac unit within minutes where many lives were saved, so had she already had the death of someone she loved to come to terms with?

He wasn't to know that what she'd said referred to the living as well as the dead. That he was the one who had been lost to her for five long years and sadly nothing had changed all that much since his return, except that now she cared for him more than ever.

As a winter dawn was breaking a cardiac consultant came to tell them that for the present George's heart problem was under control. He was being monitored on a twenty-four-hour basis and if they wanted to go home for a few hours there was no reason why they shouldn't.

'If you want to have a brief chat with your friend before you go, that will be fine as long as you don't stay too long,' he reminded them.

'Look after her, Dr Somerton,' George said weakly when they were about to leave the hospital and turn their attention to getting Nadine back home safely.

'I'll do my best, if she'll let me,' Aaron promised dryly, and wondered what Julianne had meant by what he'd heard her say in the ambulance. He decided he would ask her when she was calmer then went to sort out a taxi to take them the short distance to the village.

'We need breakfast before we do anything else,' he said as the main street came in sight, 'and when we have a moment we'll display a notice outside the bakery to explain why it is closed. It being Sunday, there will be no concerns regarding that today, but tomorrow there will be regular customers wondering where George is.'

CHAPTER NINE

INSTEAD of instructing the taxi driver to take them to the bakery, Aaron asked him to take them to his cottage and Julianne observed him enquiringly.

'I'm going to make you breakfast,' he said. 'You've been awake half the night and need time to unwind.'

'But what about Nadine?' she questioned. 'I shouldn't have left George either. He wouldn't have left me if it had been the other way round.'

'Nonsense! You heard what he said, Julianne. He told me to look after you and that is what I'm going to do. There is no better place he could be than on the coronary unit, so I am going to feed you and then you can catch up on your sleep for a couple of hours or even longer before you go home to get ready for this afternoon. Remember it isn't until we've done our Sunday shift that we will be taking your sister home. There should be plenty of time to unwind.'

'Yes, but I haven't packed,' she told him. 'I need several changes of clothes and my nurse's uniform, and the moment I get back to the bakery the notice must go up explaining about George's illness.'

They had arrived at their destination and Aaron paid the taxi driver. When he'd driven off he said, 'I'll see to the notice when I take you there, but first let's eat. Do you want the full Monty, eggs, bacon, the lot, or just cereal and toast? But before I start, can I ask you something?'

'It depends what it is,' she told him, wondering what was coming next.

'It's with regard to what I heard you say in the ambulance about losing those you love. Have you lost someone at some time in your life, like I lost my parents? Been bereaved and were afraid it might happen again to someone that you care about?'

'No, I've never had someone close to me die,' she said slowly, 'but there are other ways of losing the people we love.' A vision came to mind of him standing at the altar beside Nadine with her close by, desolate as she watched the man that she so desperately wanted to notice *her* prepare to make his wedding vows to her sister, and again an opportunity was presenting itself to tell him what had been in her heart that day, but instead she said, 'I'd rather not discuss it, Aaron, if you don't mind. It was a long time ago.'

'Yes, sure,' he agreed, and wondered if it was a love affair that had gone wrong. That it was why someone as beautiful as she had no wedding or engagement ring on her finger.

But he had brought her here to eat and pointing himself in the direction of the kitchen paused to ask, 'So which is it to be, cereal and toast or something more filling?'

'Just cereal and toast please,' she replied, and he left her sitting silently beside the wood-burning stove that kept the breakfast room warm and welcoming on winter days.

When he came back with the food she was asleep, with dark lashes sweeping her cheek bones, curled up like a defenceless infant in the womb, and the thought came to him from out of nowhere how alone she was, surrounded by friends and acquaintances and with a family of sorts in the background, but alone when it came to someone to cherish her, to be a rock to hold on to.

As if aware of his gaze on her, Julianne opened her eyes suddenly and stared up at him, observing him blankly as if she'd lost her bearings, then she was sitting upright and smiling at the sight of the food that he'd prepared set out on a table nearby, and in keeping with his thoughts about her she said, 'I'm not used to being looked after like this, Aaron, except by George maybe.' As the smile was replaced by concern, she went on, 'When I've eaten, may I use your phone to call the coronary unit to check on his condition?'

'Yes, of course,' he said. 'Anything that will make you happy is yours for the asking.' She wondered if he knew that he was treading on dangerous ground. What would he say if she asked him to make love to her or, even more preposterous, to marry her?

After all, there was no other woman in his life that she was aware of, except Nadine maybe, and he'd tuned in to her fears about that with scornful amazement.

The report on George was good. Because they'd brought him into hospital fast he was still responding well to treatment and as she listened to what was being said at the other end of the line Julianne felt relief wash over her in a welcoming tide.

'So?' Aaron enquired when she'd finished the call. 'Have we good news?'

'Yes, indeed!' she told him. 'They are pleased with his progress but it's early days yet. At least I can go to stay with Nadine until he is discharged and then leave her for a while to take care of him.'

'And in the middle of all that, on your feet at the practice from eight-thirty until six-thirty every week-day, I think not! I will help all I can, but Christmas is only a short time away as well, isn't it? Reminders of it are appearing all the time in Swallowbrook and around the lake, and as it will be my first Christmas in the lakes for five years it's something that I'm really looking forward to.

'They tell me at the practice that the surgery staff go for a Christmas meal every year in early December at the big hotel on the lakeside.'

'Yes, they do, but I don't know how easy that will be for me this time,' she told him. 'It will all depend on how Nadine is. I can't leave her alone in her big house when everyone else is celebrating.'

'Problem solved,' he said easily. 'We'll take her with us.'

He'd just described the two of them as 'we' and 'us'.

How much had he meant of the closeness that it conjured up? Was that how he saw them, or was it just a casual description that meant virtually nothing?

Changing the subject, she asked, 'Have you thought any more about buying this beautiful house?'

He could have told her that he'd thought of nothing else but *her* and *it* ever since he'd told her about the place being up for sale, but she'd put such a dampener on it with her warnings and lack of interest that he'd almost decided not to bother.

Yet now having Julianne sitting across the breakfast table from him, the adrenaline surge that the news of it being on the market had created the first time was back.

'Yes, I've thought about it a lot,' he replied, 'but haven't yet made any moves in that direction.' He wondered what she would say if she knew that it all depended on her whether he made an offer for The Falls Cottage.

With the news on George still reassuring and it being hours before they were due at the hospice, Aaron persuaded Julianne to go back to her place by the fire and catch up on the rest she'd lost while he did a few chores, and every time he gazed at her sleeping peacefully he thought how right she seemed there, curled up in his home, in his life, *in his heart*.

Later they went back to the bakery and while he sorted out the notice to announce the bakery closure Julianne packed all the things she was going to need at

Fellside. A place that was missing its master and about to see the return of its much-chastened mistress, who was sorely missing the goose that laid the golden eggs. And Howie was not aware that she'd tried to give him the child he'd demanded, but without success.

When Julianne and Aaron arrived at the hospice in the early afternoon they were surprised to find the bed in the private ward empty and the wardrobe where Nadine's clothes had hung was in a similar state.

'Where is my sister?' she asked a nurse who had seen them arrive and come in search of them.

'She has gone home already,' she was told. 'Her husband came for her.'

'Her husband! He hasn't been around for weeks. That was why Nadine was in such low spirits.'

The nurse smiled. 'Then he must have been the tonic she was short of. She has left you a letter, Julianne, and requests that you read it when you're alone. It's there on the bedside table.'

'Nothing changes, does it?' Aaron said grimly. 'She could at least have waited to see you before she went.'

'Yes, I know,' she said softly. She could live with that, but could he? Did he see Nadine leaving without saying goodbye as a repeat of that other occasion? Nadine doing what she did best, looking after number one, but at least this time it was she, Julianne, who was in the firing line and she was more used to Nadine's lack of thought for others than he was.

It was time for them to make their appearance on the wards and he was already turning to go, ready to give his time to those who would need him during the next few hours. There was the letter on the table that needed to be read, but not now. It would have to wait until a better moment presented itself. If she didn't appear on the ward on time they would be marking her down as absent.

'So what's the story?' Aaron asked when they met up again at the end of the afternoon. 'Have you had time to read the letter?'

'Er, yes,' she said calmly. 'I managed to read it while we were having a cup of tea when all was quiet for a few moments.' Her voice softened. 'You never told me that you'd been trying to trace Howie ever since we found Nadine was a patient here. How did you manage to find him, Aaron?'

'Through his business interests mainly. I know someone in the same line as him and through some careful enquiries discovered that he was in China, setting up a company there, and wasn't in contact with anyone over here, *including* his wife.

'He got in touch with me a couple of days ago and when he heard about Nadine's physical state and the loss of the baby, he tied up all the ends at the place where he was and said he would be home soon.'

'And you didn't think to tell me any of this?' she enquired gently.

'It was to be a surprise, an end to your concerns about your sister, but the guy moved faster than I expected with his homecoming arrangements, it would seem. However, getting back to the present, are you going to tell me what Nadine said in the letter?'

'Some of it, yes. It was mainly to thank us for being there for her when she needed someone so desperately, and a promise that they would be in touch soon.

'She says that she can't exist away from the lifestyle that she's grown accustomed to, that she and her husband are reconciled and are going to try for another baby soon. How do you feel about that?'

'Glad to hear it. Surely you didn't expect me to feel otherwise?' he said abruptly, passing her the outdoor jacket that she'd travelled in. 'Let's go and have a coffee somewhere and then visit George. You'd like that, wouldn't you?'

'Yes,' she said, sparkling up at him.

She pushed to the back of her mind some of the things that Nadine had said, which he wasn't going to hear, such as, *'You are the only member of the Marshall family who hasn't always got an eye to the main chance, Julianne. Why don't you just for once see what is in front of you and do something about it? Aaron Somerton is even more dishy now than he was when I had my change of mind, and you and he fit in so much better than he and I ever did. You must be blind if you can't see that!'*

She saw it all right, but did he? She doubted it. He was attracted to her, she had no doubt about that, but their history when she'd seen what Nadine had done to him and had seemed to approve had done nothing to endear her to him, and though their attraction to each other could be mind-blowing if they let it take over, there would always be the dark past to eat away at their contentment.

It would be easy enough to tell him why she'd behaved like she had that day, to confess that she'd been filled with longing for him and had been grateful that he had been spared her sister's selfishness and unreliability, but his rage and the fact that she, the bridesmaid and younger sister, had been a nonentity as far as he'd been concerned would have made her choke in the telling of it.

Now, in maturity, she could face bringing her feelings out into the open, except for one thing, she still wanted him desperately. Nothing had changed that, but would Aaron ever feel the same about her, and if he did would it be the kind of love that hers was…*eternal, until the end of time*?

George was delighted to see them and came up with the information that painkillers were keeping him free of the distress he'd experienced at the onset of his heart failure, and that they'd assured him on the unit that the abnormal heart rhythms he had experienced were not unusual, that it was only when a certain kind of abnormality known as ventricular fibrillation had interfered with the heart's pumping process that there was danger of a fatality if there was a delay in getting the patient to hospital.

'And I haven't got anything like that,' he told them, 'so I should be home soon.'

He didn't know much about what was happening with Julianne's sister so didn't make any enquiries regarding her, but when the bell rang to say that visiting time was over she said, 'I'll be in to see you after work tomorrow, George.'

'Don't neglect your sister because of me,' he protested. 'You won't have time to come here as well as go to the hospice in the evenings.'

'She's back home with her husband.' she told him, and Aaron by her side commented dryly, 'Praise be for that!'

As they drove the short distance back to the village he said, 'I don't like the idea of you being alone during the night above that big barn of a bakery. I've got a spare room at my place that you can use until George comes home if you want.'

She swallowed hard. It *would* be a bit spooky on her own above the bakery building with George not around, but could she stand being so close to yet so far from Aaron during the long winter nights without letting him see how much she would want to lie with him instead of occupying the spare room?

Without giving herself time to change her mind, she said, 'Thanks for the offer. You are so good to me, but I think I should have bed and breakfast at the pub for a few nights. They are nearly always booked up, but they know me well enough at The Mallard and I'm sure they'll be able to find me a corner somewhere.'

'So that is what you would prefer, is it?' he asked

coolly, 'staying in a noisy pub rather than under *my* roof? I don't sleepwalk, or snore, and certainly I'm not in the habit of ravishing any women guests in the middle of the night. Maybe you'd like it better if I did.'

'Now you are being offensive,' she told him with her hackles rising, 'and The Mallard is not just a pub. It's a delightful Lakeland inn and is where I'm going to stay.'

'So be it,' he said grimly as it came in sight. 'As your cases are still in the boot from when we thought you were going to be moving in with Nadine, do you want to go in and book a room? Once that is done I'll carry them up for you?'

'Yes, I suppose so,' she agreed, and left him in the car while she went to enquire if they had a single room available as it was a popular place with the tourists who came to the lakes and fells all the year round.

She emerged with the news that they had a room vacant in the roof space and as Aaron transferred her belongings to an attic that was far from sumptuous he had to restrain himself from commenting on its pokiness.

As he was about to depart, with the atmosphere still cool between them, he pointed to a window in the roof space and said, 'In case of emergency, that would be a good means of escape.'

'Are you serious?' she exclaimed. 'What sort of an emergency do you have in mind?'

'The kind that is less likely to occur at The Falls Cottage than in this place,' came his the reply, 'but I'm going, Julianne, and will see you in the morning at the practice. It's good that you don't have the long drive from the stately home in front of you to get there. So we do have Nadine to thank for one thing.'

They had her to thank for *two* things, Julianne thought as he went striding down the narrow stairs that led from the attic room. The advice she'd offered in her letter was the other, but the trouble was it sounded so easy on paper to throw caution to the winds and let Aaron see how much she loved him when after all she *was* a Marshall.

He'd had a nasty experience with her sister, had heard nothing good about her parents, and although Nadine was prepared to admit that Julianne was the only one of the family who didn't always put self first, Aaron had no proof of that, and in any case she'd spoilt the closeness that had been developing between them by refusing his offer of the spare room, which would have been a much more pleasant place to sleep than this room.

She would have felt that she belonged there more than in the only room that had been vacant at the pub, but for a feeling of belonging one had to belong, and if that ever happened she would die from the joy of it.

So for now it had to be the attic room that had resulted in her almost falling out with Aaron who had been there for her every step of the way since George had been taken ill and they'd found Nadine gone.

He had looked after her needs, cared for her in distress, and because he'd wanted her safe for the night had suggested she stay where she would come to no harm, but instead she'd got herself all steamed up at the thought of them spending the night beneath the same roof and had opted for bed and breakfast at The Mallard.

It was still early evening, too soon to go to bed, where she was certain to lie sleepless for hours, going over the day that was past with its peaks and valleys. With a sudden longing to be where there was light and cheer, she put on her favourite red dress and went to sit by the big log fire downstairs with a glass of wine.

'Julianne!' a voice cried from the doorway just minutes later. 'Where have you been? We haven't seen you for ages.'

It was one of the guys from the group she went around with and behind him were the rest of her friends greeting her cheerfully. Within minutes they were all laughing and chatting together around a big table, except for one of the men who had gone to get the drinks.

When Aaron stopped the car on the drive of the cottage he stayed in the driving seat, unmoving. He shouldn't have gone stamping off and left Julianne like he had. There was all the rest of the evening to come and he'd left her there out on a limb after what had not been a good day.

If he hadn't been so keen to show her that he wasn't pleased at her refusal of his offer of the spare room they could have spent the evening together in the pub, which would have been so much better than both of them alone and miserable, because that was what he was now.

He backed out onto the road again, knowing that he wouldn't rest until he'd seen her once more, and drove back to where he'd left her with a dismal vision of her cooped in that ghastly room with no one to talk to.

When he arrived he could tell that the place was filling up with the evening clientele. There were more cars in the car park, more noise issuing forth from the building, and he went inside with one purpose in mind—to make peace with Julianne.

That determination lasted until he saw her surrounded by those he'd seen her with that night when he'd first come to Swallowbrook. She was stunning in the same red dress and was the centre of attention as she sparkled across at some guy who was chatting her up.

So much for the Cinderella vision he'd conjured up of her crouching over the paltry gas fire in that bedroom, he thought grimly, and turning he was out of the place in two strides because it was obvious that she had refused to stay at the cottage because she'd had other plans that hadn't included him.

'Julianne, wasn't that your doctor friend in the doorway?' one of the people she was with said suddenly, and when she looked across Aaron was disappearing into the car park from where he'd just come. By the time she'd gathered her wits and put back on the shoes she'd flung to one side to rest her feet when she'd come down from upstairs, he had his car engine running and as she came out and ran towards him in the cold night he drove off without a backwards glance.

She chased after him for a few seconds, waving for him to stop, but he ignored her efforts and as frost nipped at her bare arms and her heels slithered on it on the tarmac of the car park, she went back inside and straight up to her room, knowing that there was only one interpretation Aaron would put on what he'd seen.

He wasn't to know that her smile had been forced, that she had been laughing when the moment had demanded it and feeling so alien to what had been her life before he had come back into it that she could scarcely believe it.

She phoned him, desperate to explain what he'd seen, but received only the automated voice with the information that the person she wished to speak to was not available, and thought glumly that that was how it was going to be from now on, the man she loved was *not available*.

Monday morning had come round again and as Julianne drove the short distance to the practice beside frost-crusted pavements she felt cold inside and out.

The outer chill was seasonal and as such welcomed. It fitted in with council workmen putting into position a large Christmas tree in front of the village hall as she went past, an early reminder of the season.

The inner chill she felt was of a different kind, the cold emptiness of rejection, and there was nothing to celebrate about *that*. But she told herself there were those who would be coming to the surgery with their minor and major health problems who were going to need her with a clear head and steady hands for the day ahead, and if she and Aaron had to pair up for any part of it she was going to let him see that she had left personal problems behind. There was no way she was going to put a foot wrong today.

He had arrived. His car was already parked outside and despite her best intentions her heartbeat quickened. The surgery was not yet open for the day's health care to commence and as she was passing the door of Aaron's consulting room he looked up from his desk and said, 'Nurse Marshall, can you spare a moment?'

'Yes, of course,' she replied, coming to a halt, and went to stand facing him reluctantly, wondering what was coming next. Was it to be a comment about the night before when he'd seen her all smiles, swanning around in the red dress, having perked up amazingly as soon as he'd gone?

It seemed that it wasn't. Aaron wasn't prepared to mix business with *dis*pleasure as he said levelly, 'I see that James Ericson is on my list of appointments for today. I'm due to give him a corticosteroid injection in his other knee to relieve acute arthritis, and if you remember the last time he came he was very difficult to deal with because he hadn't been my patient before.

'I'm told he used to be Nathan's father's patient and when John Gallagher retired he switched to his son, but as Nathan doesn't do that sort of thing and I do, he has been passed over to me. The last time I saw him I suggested that in view of the relief he'd had from the first injection I should do the other knee, which is also very painful.

'James has agreed, but not willingly as the old guy is too set in his ways to take kindly to a newcomer, so

I would like you to be present in case he needs to be charmed a little to get him off his high horse and make him more easy to deal with.'

'Yes, of course,' she agreed stiffly, and wondered if the 'charm' word was a reminder of what she'd been up to last night when he'd arrived at The Mallard unexpectedly and left grim-faced. She'd felt the need to say she was sorry ever since, but what had she done wrong?

Nothing. It had just been a fitting end to a stressful day and as Aaron seemed to have nothing else to say she went to get started in the nurse's room. The only time she saw him after that was when James appeared and was surprisingly docile, which caused her to think that maybe Aaron had just been making sure that she was earning her crust.

She went to see George that evening and it felt strange to be making the short journey to the hospital in her small runabout after all the evenings spent visiting Nadine in the hospice. Every time she did her voluntary work there from now on a vision of her sister, pale and lethargic, in the bed of the private ward would come to mind.

George's first words when he saw her were, 'Where's Dr Somerton? I'm getting used to seeing the two of you together.'

'Not any more,' she told him. 'But how are *you*? That is what I'm here for.'

'I'm improving and expect to be home by the end of the week.' Switching away from his welfare to hers, he enquired, 'Were you happy about being in the bakery on your own last night?'

'Er, no, not exactly,' she explained. 'Aaron wanted me to stay at The Falls Cottage but I opted for bed and breakfast at The Mallard.'

'And is that why he's not here?'

She flashed him a wry smile. 'It could be, I suppose, but I haven't come to talk about that. It's six weeks to Christmas and festive fever is beginning to sweep over Swallowbrook.

'The surgery staff are going for the meal that Laura is arranging on the first of December and this year those employed in Gabriel's cancer clinic next to the surgery will be joining us.'

'And your doctor friend will he be there?'

'I would imagine so,' she replied flatly, and hoped that a certain pharmaceutical rep wouldn't be there. She'd had her sights set on Hugo until she'd discovered that his heart belonged to Ruby.

Back at The Falls Cottage Aaron was debating how to spend the evening. With Julianne on the fringe of his life once more, he was realising how much she meant to him and admitting that he had no right to tell her what to do with her free time.

If they'd been engaged and he'd walked in on her as she'd been last night he might have had something to get heated about, but not under the present circumstances.

The ring was still there in its box, waiting to be pro-duced. What better time than Christmas to tell Julianne how much he loved her? But the moment had gone because he'd loved her too much and let pique come between them.

CHAPTER TEN

NOVEMBER had gone, taking with it the usual grey days and unexciting nights of the month, and December had arrived with tinsel and toys, mulled wine in the shops, and restaurants eager for early bookings of their Christmas fare.

With all the signs of the most popular festival of the year around her Julianne was finding it difficult to raise any enthusiasm because Aaron was still where he had placed himself on the edge of her life, and it looked as if he intended to stay there.

Added to that, George was home, having made a good recovery but talking about selling the business and retiring, and that could mean an end to her contentment above the bakery.

The first day of the month was a Saturday. The Christmas meal that the practice manager had arranged for the staff was to take place that evening and as Julianne observed the contents of her wardrobe she thought that, whatever she decided to wear, it would *not* be the red dress.

Something black maybe to fit in with her mood, or a turquoise silk number that she was fond of, anything but red. She still shuddered at the thought of what she must have looked like when Aaron had come back to The Mallard unexpectedly.

Shoeless, shameless, he'd probably thought, *and not to be missed in scarlet*! If he hadn't been sure if she was like the rest of her family, he would be now. After leaving her looking pale and washed out after a stressful day, he'd gone back to be there for her the rest of the evening, only to find that the Marshall in her *had* surfaced and she was back on top form, like she'd been when he'd first arrived in Swallowbrook.

But if he had thought any, or all, of that, he had prejudged her, she felt, with tears pricking. She'd gone down to find warmth and light below without any other thought in mind and it was only when her friends had come strolling in that she'd felt the need to put on a good face. They'd rarely seen her downcast and she hadn't wanted to be asked questions that she hadn't wanted to have to answer.

Since then the only connection between Aaron and herself had been on medical matters at the surgery and of one thing she was sure, she would not be the life and soul of the party tonight. So out of the wardrobe came the demure turquoise number. If she'd had a nun's habit, she might have worn that!

She was the last to arrive, having left the ordeal to the last moment, and, sure enough, when she got there the pharmaceutical rep who'd had designs on Hugo and had had to back off was hovering around Aaron like the limpet she was, so with a brief nod in his direction Julianne went to find where she had been placed at the dining table and discovered that it was next to him, which would be a conversation stopper if ever there was one.

'Why were you so late?' he asked as everyone began to take their places for the meal. 'I was beginning to think you weren't coming.'

'I have to admit I was undecided… Would it have mattered if I hadn't?' she asked in a low voice that was for his ears only.

'I would expect you to know the answer to that.'

'Yes, well, I don't, I'm afraid.' The hurt of the moment brought the sting of tears. She forced them back and turned to speak to the person seated on the other side of her, who happened to be Nathan's father, John, long retired from the practice but still with a great interest in the health care that it provided for the village and surrounding areas, while he lived contentedly in a pinewood lodge on a river bank not far away, where he spent most of his time fishing.

Further along the table was Laura Armitage, the practice manager who had masterminded the Christmas gathering, and beside her Gabriel, her charismatic husband.

Opposite them were Ruby and Hugo Lawrence, who were soon to adopt a baby.

There was happiness everywhere Julianne looked and she wished that her Christmas was going to be as delightful as theirs, but with Aaron still on the edge of her life the chances of that were slim.

'Do you want to dance?' he asked when the meal was over and they had all toasted the practice and the cancer clinic and were congregating in the area of the hotel ballroom and the bar.

Of course she wanted to dance. There was nothing she enjoyed more when she was out with her friends, but dancing with Aaron was a different matter. He had most likely asked her because the social butterfly that he thought she was would want to be seen and admired, and what better place to give her that pleasure than on the dance floor?

He was observing her with raised brows as no reply was immediately forthcoming, and said, 'It is what you enjoy most, isn't it?'

'I like dancing, yes, I always have, but it doesn't rule my life.' Pointing to an empty table on the edge of the dance floor, she told him, 'I will be quite happy just *watching* the dancing, thanks just the same.'

'The reason being that either you don't think I will be up to your standard after exiling myself in Africa for the last five years? Or you don't want anything more to do with me?' he questioned dryly.

'Neither of those things!' she protested unsteadily. 'I just don't want any more hurt.'

'Not from me surely!' he exclaimed. 'When have *I* ever hurt *you*, Julianne?'

'You haven't…' she gulped '…but just knowing you has been hurtful. Do you remember at the wedding when you accused me of being happy when Nadine ran off and left you?'

'Yes, I remember only too well. I'm hardly likely to forget any of the happenings of that day, but it wasn't me that was dishing out the hurt, was it? Why hark back to that? And if we are going to start bringing skeletons out of the cupboard, I suggest that we do it in private.'

Taking her arm, he led her away from the rest of the surgery staff to where there was one of many small terraces overlooking the lake that was unoccupied. Seating her on one of the sofas that it was furnished with, he stood looking down at her thoughtfully and said, 'You were saying?'

'Yes, I was,' she breathed, with hands tightly clasped. 'It is true that I didn't want Nadine to marry you.'

'Why, for God's sake?'

'There were two reasons.'

'And they were?' he asked grimly.

'First of all I knew she would hurt you and deceive you. That at the same time the two of you were planning to marry she was seeing someone else regularly. I didn't know his name, had never seen him, yet he was there in the background all right and was wealthy.'

'I see. And the other reason why you weren't sorry to see me left high and dry at the altar?'

She took a deep breath. 'I wanted you to love *me* instead.'

'*Whaaat?* The young sister who I wouldn't have known if I'd passed her in the street in love with *me*!'

He sank down on to the seat beside her and said

dazedly, 'I suppose we all have childish crushes at some time or another when we're young. I certainly had no knowledge of that. I wouldn't have ranted at you in the church vestry that day if I had.

'When I next saw you, working at the practice, I wouldn't have recognised you as the bridesmaid because you had changed so much. It was only when I heard your name that it dawned on me that you were a member of the family that you warned me about not so long ago.'

'Maybe I warned you too well.'

'What do you mean?'

'I mean that when you came back to The Mallard the other night you soon found a brush to tar me with. I had gone downstairs looking for light and warmth away from that grotty room, and no sooner had I done so than some of my friends appeared and my smiles and laughter were for their benefit. I haven't seen much of them since you'd been around and I didn't want any awkward questions coming my way.

'After you wouldn't stop for me when I tried to flag you down, I went back up there and went to bed with the feeling that I'd just been found wanting, and that feeling is still there.'

Nathan appeared at that moment and said, 'Libby is going to relieve the childminder, and having noted that neither of you have brought your cars, she's asking if either or both of you want a lift home now?'

Aaron shook his head. There was no way he wanted to leave Julianne at that moment. It was true what she'd said about his reactions when he'd seen her at The Mallard that night. For a few fleeting moments he had labelled her with the same description as the rest of her family, and it had been totally unfair. As soon as Nathan had gone he was going to put things right between them for ever.

But it didn't work out like that. She forestalled him by telling Nathan, 'I would be grateful for a lift.' She turned to him, and he was taken aback by the quick escape route she'd found for herself. 'Bye for now, Aaron.'

After that clear indication that for her the night was over as far as they were concerned, he went back to join the rest of the party still stunned by what she'd told him. She'd cared for him *then*, but what about *now*? There had been a large gap in their lives between the two.

He needed to tell Julianne that to him she would always be her delightful self, not labelled as a member of a family who seemed to do as they pleased with each other's feelings.

The night when he'd gone back to The Mallard and seen her in an apparently happy mood, his annoyance had been more along the lines of pique. Because he'd left her tired and dejected and the moment she'd seen her friends Julianne had brightened up, something she hadn't been able to do with him.

With Nadine back where she belonged without a goodbye, and George far from well with his heart condition, he'd been totally protective of her, to the point of asking her to stay at his place for safety's sake. Her refusal had lit the spark of his annoyance when she'd opted for The Mallard instead, and when he'd gone back with his concern for her unabated and found her smiling as if she hadn't a care in the world, the spark had become a flame fuelled by angry disbelief, until tonight.

His mouth softened at the memory of how she'd confessed to being in love with him all those years ago. He hoped that time and absence would not have changed that when he asked Julianne to marry him. Yet there had been no mention of it being an ongoing affection. She would surely have said if it was, or would she not want to risk a rebuff? They hadn't exactly been in tune over recent days.

She'd done it! She'd cleared the air about her feelings for him on the non-event that was to have been his wedding day. Aaron knew now that there had been no deceit or conniving on her part, that her only crime had been in wanting him.

It had been noticeable during those few painful moments when she'd been telling him what *her* feelings had been on the worst day of his life, that he'd shown no urgency to discover if her love for him had survived, and Libby's offer of a lift, even though the evening was only half-over, had come just at the right moment.

It was an hour later and she was debating what to do next. Did she want to stay at the practice, knowing that every time she felt Aaron's glance on her she was going to feel she'd put herself at a disadvantage through her confession of earlier in the evening?

He'd obviously been touched by it, but it hadn't altered the fact that she was still one of a family who were never there when she needed them. Nothing was going to change that, and if in the past she'd managed to forget it sometimes, having Nadine now living so near was going to change that.

When the intercom buzzed suddenly into the silence, her heart skipped a beat. When it sounded again she went slowly to answer it and Aaron's voice filled the room.

'Let me in, Julianne,' he said. 'There's something I want to say to you.'

Without replying, she released the catch on the downstairs door and within seconds could hear him bounding up the stairs.

'Back at the hotel you said that you loved me once,' he said, without any of the niceties when he came striding into the room.

Speechless, she nodded.

'That was then. It didn't last? Absence didn't make the heart grow fonder?'

He was firing the questions at her as if she was being interviewed for a position and when he produced a small velvet box and lifted the lid to reveal the diamond ring that he'd been longing to put on her finger, it was a fitting description of the moment.

'I've never loved anyone else, Aaron, if that is what you want me to say,' she said in a low voice. 'The long absence didn't make me love you more because I thought I would never see you again. It was only when I heard that you were coming to work in the practice and going to live in Swallowbrook that I knew just how much I longed to be near you again.'

He was smiling and it lit up the dark hazel eyes looking into hers, 'So will you marry me, Julianne?' He took the diamond ring out of its box. 'And wear my ring? Soon I'll put a gold band beside it to tell the world that you're mine. I've wanted you from the moment I saw you that day in the surgery and realised who you were. You were so beautiful and full of life.'

'And you think you'll be able to cope with your in-laws?' she said laughingly.

'Just watch me,' he promised. 'I'll even be godfather to this child that Nadine's going to have one day to please old moneybags, that's if I'm asked, of course.'

'Yes, I'll marry you, Aaron,' she said softly. 'I feel as if I've been waiting for this day for ever.'

He held out his arms and said, 'Then come here where you belong. The waiting is over for both of us, only the future matters from now on.' After that there was a long silence in the small apartment above the bakery until he said, 'I've bought The Falls Cottage. How do you fancy living next to a waterfall?'

'Fine,' she told him, glowing with the joy he had brought. 'Wherever you are is where I will always want to be.'

EPILOGUE

I<small>T WAS</small> the morning of New Year's Day after the most fantastic Christmas of their lives, filled with joy, laughter and sweet promises, and a wedding was to take place in the village church.

The bride was to be given away by her father, who had suddenly decided that he was ready to live on dry land for a while, and her mother was going to be there too, having coaxed her second husband to bring her back to her own country for a prolonged holiday.

Her sister wasn't sure she if she would be joining them as she was experiencing a lot of morning sickness, but she and her husband had been invited to join the wedding party if they so wished.

The church bells had been pealing out across the Lakeland village since the middle of the morning and now it was midday, time for Julianne and Aaron to make their lifelong commitments to each other, and as she walked sedately down the aisle on her father's arm in a wedding dress that was exquisite in its simplicity, the first flakes of snow of the New Year began to fall from the sky.

There had been a scattering of them on the day of
the crowning of the Snow Queen, but this was the real
thing, just as the wedding that was to take place was the
real thing for the bridegroom standing straight and tall
at the altar and for his beautiful bride who had loved
and lost and loved again, this time for ever.

Seated not far away from them, George wiped a tear
from his eye. He had gone ahead with his plans to retire
and would shortly be moving into one of the pine lodges
near that of John Gallagher, but before hanging up his
baker's hat and apron he had made their wedding cake
for Julianne and Aaron and now it stood proudly in the
centre of the top table at the reception that was to take
place at the hotel after the wedding.

All the staff from the practice were there to wish
them every happiness in their life together, and as they
said the ageless words of their wedding vows, promis-
ing to have and to hold, to love and to cherish, they both
knew that was how it was going to be, and now Aaron
was keeping the promise he had made to Julianne on
that night in the apartment when it had all come together for them. The gold band of marriage was taking
its place beside the diamond.

* * * * *

MILLS & BOON Book Club — 2 Free Books!

Get your free books now at
www.millsandboon.co.uk/freebookoffer

Or fill in the form below and post it back to us

THE MILLS & BOON® BOOK CLUB™—HERE'S HOW IT WORKS: Accepting your free books places you under no obligation to buy anything. You may keep the books and return the despatch note marked 'Cancel'. If we do not hear from you, about a month later we'll send you 5 brand-new stories from the Medical™ series, including two 2-in-1 books priced at £5.49 each and a single book priced at £3.49*. There is no extra charge for post and packaging. You may cancel at any time, otherwise we will send you 5 stories a month which you may purchase or return to us—the choice is yours. *Terms and prices subject to change without notice. Offer valid in UK only. Applicants must be 18 or over. Offer expires 31st July 2013. **For full terms and conditions, please go to www.millsandboon.co.uk/freebookoffer**

Mrs/Miss/Ms/Mr (please circle) _____

First Name _____

Surname _____

Address _____

_____

_____ Postcode _____

E-mail _____

Send this completed page to: Mills & Boon Book Club, Free Book Offer, FREEPOST NAT 10298, Richmond, Surrey, TW9 1BR

Find out more at
www.millsandboon.co.uk/freebookoffer

Visit us Online

0712/M2YEA

Special Offers

Every month we put together collections and longer reads written by your favourite authors.

Here are some of next month's highlights— and don't miss our fabulous discount online!

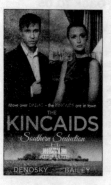

On sale 15th February   On sale 15th February   On sale 1st March

Save 20% on all Special Releases

Find out more at
www.millsandboon.co.uk/specialreleases

Visit us Online

0313/ST/MB407